THIS
BOOK
BELONGS
TO

CAMELOT BARBARA BRENNER was born in Brooklyn and attended Rutgers and New York University. She has worked for the publications division of the Bank Street College of Education. Mrs. Brenner has published a number of books for children. She and her illustrator husband, Fred Brenner, have two sons and live in West Nyack, New York.

A Year In The Life Of Rosie Bernard

Barbara Brenner

CAMELOT BOOKS/PUBLISHED BY AVON

AVON BOOKS
A division of
The Hearst Corporation
959 Eighth Avenue
New York, New York 10019

First Camelot Printing, February, 1974.

CAMELOT TRADEMARK REG. U.S. PAT. OFF.
AND IN OTHER COUNTRIES,
MARCA REGISTRADA, HECHO EN U.S.A.

Printed in the U.S.A.

To May Garelick,
my first editor, my good friend

Contents

A year in the life of

❀ ❀ Rosie Bernard

1 ❀ ❀ ❀ ARRIVAL

1932. NIGHT. And it was snowing. You could see the snowflakes against the light from the streetlamps. The horse's hooves made a soft clopping noise as the milk wagon rumbled along the snow-covered street.

It was an ordinary enough *looking* milk wagon. Like a dozen you could have seen on the streets of Brooklyn in those days. It was pulled by a patient old gray horse, and driven by an elderly man with a bushy moustache who clucked his tongue and yelled "Hup" at the horse from time to time. As if he were anxious to finish his route and get all the milk delivered to the housewives of Flatbush.

But—the thing about this particular wagon was—there was no milk in it. Not one Grade-A drop. Instead, if you'd looked inside you'd have seen, alongside the empty milk boxes and the extra horse blanket,

a battered old blue theatrical trunk,

a small red suitcase,

a few parcels tied with string . . .

And a girl.

She was sitting on one of the milk boxes, wrapped in a large plaid shawl. A few wisps of brown hair had escaped from under the shawl, and this, along with a pair of green eyes in a thin face and a pair of skinny legs in woolen stockings, was about all you could see of her.

But something in the way she sat there told you that for her this was no ordinary journey— the faraway look in her eyes, the way she chewed absentmindedly on a stray strand of hair, everything about her said, *worry, heavy trouble, deep thought*. . . .

How funny the horse's hooves sound from here inside the wagon . . . such a steady beat, like a word, over and over. . . . clop, clop clop clop clop clop . . . going going going. . . . That's it, Rosie Bernard. Think about where you're going, not where you've been. Never look back.

That's what Daddy said. . . . OK. . . . I'm in Grandpa's milk wagon, and he's taking me to live in Brooklyn with him and Grandma and my cousins and aunts and uncles, and I'll be going to a new school and meeting new friends and learning to play stickball. So you say, Daddy. But the question is, can I believe what you say? You're also the one who said we were going to stick together through thick and thin. When Mama died you said that. But here it is barely eight months later and you're leaving me. You say it's because of Hard Times, and an actor has to take work where he can get it. All the same, a promise is a promise. I need you. And who will teach me the rest of Lady Macbeth's sleepwalking scene? Answer me that. . . . First Mama left me and now you're leaving. . . . Clop clop you could make up a poem to that sound. . . . Mama is dead . . . dead in her bed. . . . dead . . . dead . . . from a cold in the head. . . . No. It was pneumonia. Pneumonia doesn't rhyme with anything. . . . Mama played the part of someone dying in lots of plays. But real life isn't like plays. In real life you never know your part. You don't know how to act when your mother dies. . . . What did I do with those dopey pres-

ents Daddy gave me? Oh, here they are. A magnifying glass and a compass, for pete's sake. Just like Daddy to give a person dopey presents like these. What was it he said? "The compass is so you'll never get lost, even in Brooklyn." That was supposed to be funny. And the magnifying glass is so I'll learn to look at everything and give it the closest scrutiny before I make up my mind about it. "Closest scrutiny," for pete's sake. . . . Daddy. Funny Daddy. I miss you already. Three months until I see you is a long time. . . . I know. . . . The show must go on. Don't look where you've been, only where you're going. . . .

Rosie poked her head out of the wagon.

"Grandpa!"

The man with the bushy moustache turned around.

"Well, well. Look who's here. I thought you were asleep."

"Nope. Can't. Too many things to think about. When will we be there?"

"Five minutes."

"Can I come up with you?"

"Sure. Climb up. Bring the blanket. It's cold."

Rosie climbed up and settled herself next to her grandfather. She tucked the blanket around her knees, then turned to him and said, "Grandpa?"

"Yes, Liebchen."

"Is blood thicker than water?"

"What kind of question is that?"

"I mean will I like them and will they like me because we're *relatives*?"

"Nope. You'll like one another for another reason."

"What reason?"

"Because you're all fine people."

"But . . . Gramps . . . the problem is, I'm not *like* other kids my age. It's from traveling with Mama and Daddy so much. I'm different. I've never been with other children. And, besides, I'm too tall," she said desperately, as if there were a standard test for the way ten-year-old girls were supposed to be and she had failed it.

Her grandfather tried to reassure her.

"Look. Everyone's different. That's the nice thing about people. You happen to be a rare specimen. Your cousins will appreciate that. Mark my words. They're not exactly common-garden-variety kids themselves. You'll see."

Silence.

"Grandpa?"

"What now?"

"There's one thing. I *won't* go to church."

"Well, that's for you to decide. I'm not much for church myself."

"You know why I won't go. Because I'm half Jewish."

"I know."

"What does that mean, anyway? Which half of me is Jewish? Are half my cells Jewish and half of them Protestant?"

Her grandfather chuckled. "No. Nothing like that. Just means your papa is Jewish and your mother wasn't. But you can make up your own mind what you want to be."

Silence.

"Grandpa?"

"Yah."

"The problem is I'm scared."

"I know. Don't be. It'll all work out. Grandma will teach you how to make strudel, and I'll make a garden for you. And the kids . . ."

"Tell more. Hurry. Before we get there tell what it will be like."

"Well . . . the house is big. It has a flat roof you can walk out on, and on a clear day you can see all the way to Coney Island. . . . Soon it'll be time to decorate the Christmas tree, and everyone helps Grandma make gingerbread cookies . . . you won't be so lonely. . . ."

"I wasn't lonely when I had Mama and Daddy. How many people did you say live in the house?"

"Nine. Ten, with you."

"That's a lot of people to get used to."

"You got used to me petty quick. So it's only eight. . . . Rosie?"

"Yes, Gramps."

"Listen. Everybody wanted you to come. *Everybody*. You hear me?"

"Yes, Grandpa."

Silence.

And then suddenly the old man was calling "Whoa," and the horse was stopping. They had arrived.

Rosie peered from the wagon and saw a house looming out of the darkness. She could just make out the wide veranda and stone steps, and the stained-glass doors that led to the vestibule. Lights streamed from all three floors; it was as if the house were expecting someone.

"See. They're all waiting for you. Come on. We'll get your baggage later."

"Oh. Do I look all right? What should I do? What should I say? What are my cousins' names again?"

"Say what you feel. No more, no less. You look fine. Peter. Gretchen. Katie."

They went up the stone steps hand in hand. When they rang the downstairs bell, the sound echoed through the halls. And then there was the noise of running feet, the door opened wide, and Rosie found herself face to face with her new life—five grown-ups and three children whom she'd never seen before. Eight smiling faces. Rosie paused a moment on the threshold. And then she said something which was typically Rosie.

"Hullo, everybody," she said. "Due to circumstances beyond my control, I'm here."

And that is how Rosie came to Brooklyn.

2 ❀ ❀ RELATIVES

"Do you realize that I've been here two weeks, three days and fourteen hours?"

Rosie lay on her back on the parlor carpet, squinting up at the Christmas tree through her magnifying glass and thinking profound thoughts, such as the one she had just passed along.

The recipients of this wisdom were her three cousins, who were also on the floor. The four children were enjoying the holiday season. Peter was directing his electric trains on a hazardous run through the new section of track. Gretchen was engrossed in the latest adventure of Elsie Dinsmore. And little Katie had made herself a house of her own under the dining-room table in the next room, and was playing mother with her new doll. There was a pleasant feeling of companionship in the air.

Minutes passed. Then Peter looked up from his trains. "Tell me, Rosie, have you gotten over the shock of transplant yet?"

The shock of transplant. That was Grandpa's phrase. One night he had explained to the children how plants suffer when they're moved from one location to another, and how you have to compensate by giving them especially good treatment. Peter had gotten the message right away. "Like Rosie," he'd said, grinning. "We have to treat her good until she gets over the shock of transplant."

Rosie thought about Peter's question. Was she over it? "I guess I am," she said slowly. "I don't have that awful feeling at night anymore."

"Good. You don't know what a strain it's been on us having to be so nice to you. Now we can relax and be ourselves again." Peter grinned.

Gretchen looked up from her book. "Don't be such a comedian," she said. "I don't notice that you acted any different."

Rosie stayed out of the discussion. She was thinking how her cousins *had* helped, how they'd put up with her black moods, her short temper, her odd ways. From the very beginning . . .

That first night, when she'd met them. She'd never forget it. "This is Gretchen, and this is Peter, and this is our little Kate." It was as simple as that, the way they were introduced. Rosie had seen a tall, chubby boy of about twelve, a dainty dark-haired girl about her own age, and a little curly-haired moppet who stood, round-eyed, staring at Rosie with two fingers in her mouth.

Thinking back on it, she remembered Peter had winked at her and said, "She looks like a live wire." And Gretchen had smiled and said, "She'll do."

And then something had happened. They had looked at one another, and a warm, strong, familiar current had passed among them. At that moment, Rosie had thought, *We know each other. We've met before, sometime, somewhere, and now we're together again.* Then they had nodded and smiled at each other and it was over. No one would ever speak of it, yet they all knew. There was something between them.

Rosie thought about all this, lying there under the Christmas tree.

"You kids have certainly put up with a lot, having me around. Honestly," she said, caught up in the Christmas spirit, "I don't know how you *stand* me, sometimes."

"You're all right," said Gretchen generously. "It's just that you like to have your own way."

"No," said Peter. "It's not as simple as that. I think sometimes Rosie feels angry and frustrated for other reasons. What's it like not to have a mother, Rosie?"

Peter had a strange habit of asking questions like this. Putting his finger right on what was bothering you. As if he wanted you to *face* it, and think about it.

Rosie frowned, trying to decide how to answer.

"Sometimes you don't think about it at all. And sometimes it's very bad. Very bad," she added softly.

"But, at least, I have a father," she added more cheerfully.

"Yes, but he's never around, and that's almost like not having one."

"It is not." Rosie felt herself getting irritable again. Then she remembered her New Year's resolution about being easier to get along with. She picked up her compass and held it. "Daddy's a little bit south and west of here tonight," she said, changing the subject. "He's playing Philadelphia."

"What play?"

"Same one. *Hamlet*."

Peter switched off his transformer. "Is that one you've told us?"

"Yes. Remember? The one about the prince whose father is murdered, and then the ghost comes to tell him that his uncle did the murder, and then Hamlet decides to put on the play to catch the uncle and . . ."

Katie, who had been sitting quietly, listening, suddenly removed her fingers from her mouth. "To be or not to be," she said clearly.

"That's it. That's right. See. Katie remembers."

Katie almost never said anything. Gretchen claimed that her little sister was too busy thinking to be bothered with conversation. But it did seem that when Katie stirred herself to say something, she showed a remarkable grasp of what was going on.

"Tell it again. From the beginning," Peter ordered.

"In a little while." Rosie continued studying the Christmas tree. "I'm thinking right now, and I don't want to interrupt my train of thought."

"Hey! That's a great name for my new engine," said Peter. "That's what I'll call it. 'The Train of Thought.' "

The conversation subsided.

I guess I like Peter the best, Rosie mused. *He looks like that fat angel on the tree, sort of.* (She'd never say that out loud; Peter hated to be called fat.) Peter knew the *best* games. Hide-and-seek. Pirates. Sea captains. Rosie had never played any of them until she came to Brooklyn. And You-must-be. You-must-be was her favorite. It had so many possibilities. . . . You must be the Empress of Russia and I'll be Rasputin. . . . You must be Queen Elizabeth and I'll be Lord Essex. . . . You must be the cop and I'll be the robber. . . . There was no end to You-must-be. . . .

Gretchen's interests were different. Quiet

play. Monopoly and Parcheesi, checkers and dominoes, paper dolls and drawing pictures. "Go play with Gretchen and get your blood cooled down a bit," Grandma would advise, when Peter's wild games had brought Rosie indoors with flaming cheeks. Being with Gretchen could calm anyone down. And she never teased.

What about little Kate? She was sweet, but she wasn't much of a person as yet. You can't be much of a person at four. "She's still a seedling," Grandpa said. A seedling that sucks her two middle fingers, that was Katie.

Rosie's eyes continued to wander to the tree. Such a big tree. They'd had to cut some of the top off so it would fit into the first-floor parlor. It had been fun decorating it. *First time in my life I ever decorated a Christmas tree,* thought Rosie. They'd always been traveling at Christmas. Anyway, Daddy wasn't too keen on Christmas trees. Once Mama had said kiddingly that he didn't like Christmas trees because he was Jewish. "Nonsense," Daddy'd answered, "Christmas trees aren't even Christian. They're from the pagans."

Rosie didn't care where Christmas trees were from. She liked them. And this one was particularly beautiful. Grandpa had brought it all the way from the summer house in Red Hook, New York. Aunt Clementine and Aunt Gertrude had supplied the decorations from two big boxes that were brought up from the basement. Some of the ornaments were more than a hundred years old. Grandma and Grandpa had brought them from Germany.

They were a lot nicer than the ordinary Christmas balls you bought at a five-and-ten-cent store. Some of the balls were made of spun glass in the shape of peaches and berries. Others were little glass icicles that looked so real you thought they'd melt right on the rug. And others were made in the shape of angels with wings of real bird feathers.

The uncles were in charge of the lights and the aunts were the ones who directed the decorating. But everyone had helped. There had been a lot of giggling and fooling around. Aunt Clementine and Aunt Gertrude had acted like young girls. Actually, they were quite old. Probably over thirty, Rosie guessed. Aunt Clemmy was little and round and she had a mole on her cheek. Peter said that she had been a *suffragette* when she was young and had marched in parades to get the vote for women. Gretchen said her mother, Aunt Gertie, had been a *flapper*.

This had prompted a long discussion.

"All flappers did was dance the Charleston," Peter had said, rather scornfully.

"And drink gin," Rosie, who had seen a play about the Roaring Twenties, added. "Suffragettes worked for *something*."

Gretchen made an attempt to defend flappers, but finally had to agree that suffragettes were more important.

As for uncles, Rosie didn't know them well at all. At least, not yet. Uncle Lewis worked in a bank and when he came home he fell asleep behind the paper. He wore spats.

Uncle Henry, who was Peter's father, worked nights in a soda factory and smoked cigars.

"Peter," Rosie asked, just because she suddenly thought of it, "do you ever get free samples from the soda factory?"

"We used to. But now it's Hard Times."

Hard Times seemed to be everywhere. Grandpa talked a lot about it. He was worried about losing his job as a milkman; Rosie had heard him and Grandma one night as she lay in her bedroom next to theirs on the third floor. Grandpa's voice sounded angry and he said, "Mama, I'm doing my best. Don't pester me." And Grandma said something Rosie couldn't hear. And then Rosie had fallen asleep.

Grandma. Grandma was an interesting person. When Grandma spoke, everyone listened. Even the grown-ups. Aunt Gertie and Aunt Clemmy obeyed her as if they were still little girls. Of course, she was their *mother*, but still. . . .

"Don't mess around with Grandma," Peter had warned. Rosie knew what he meant. She'd had one run-in with Grandma.

It was when Rosie had first arrived. In the unpacking, she had misplaced her compass and magnifying glass. She'd been looking forward to showing them to her cousins, and as she rummaged frantically through her belongings, she got more and more annoyed. "Dammit to hell," she finally exploded. "Don't tell me I've lost them."

Grandma appeared from out of nowhere.

"Young lady," she said, her voice full of scorn, "surely you must be able to express yourself better than that. Do not *ever* let me hear you use that language in *my* house again. Do you understand?" She fixed Rosie with her special look, guaranteed to strike terror to the heart of the most intrepid.

Rosie the spunky was properly cowed. Grandma's tone had not only forbidden her to swear, but had hinted that her intelligence, her breeding, and a whole variety of other matters were on trial. Grandma, Rosie was to discover, had a knack for that.

And yet, when Rosie thought about her first days in Brooklyn, it was Grandma who came to her mind most often. Grandma coming in at night to kiss her, when she felt lonely for her father. Grandma teaching her how to bake. Grandma—talking, scolding, watching, *caring*. *She's almost like a mother*, thought Rosie.

There was one more thing that Rosie had noticed about Grandma. She was churchy. She went to church every Sunday, and read the Bible during the week, and sometimes she had the minister over in the afternoon for a Kaffeeklatsch.

"She's dying to make a Protestant out of you," Peter warned. Rosie knew it. But so far she had resisted going to church.

Every week when Grandma asked, "Rose, would you like to come to church with me today?" Rosie would reply politely, "No, thank you, Grandma. As you know, I'm half Jewish."

Grandma would close her lips tightly, but she never said anything. Once Peter said jokingly to Rosie, "Why don't you go and just stay for *half* the service!" But he said it quietly, so Grandma didn't hear.

Grandma, thought Rosie, *is a very strong-willed woman.* And then Rosie discovered one of those major truths that you find sometimes when you're lying around musing. *For pete's sake,* thought Rosie, *Grandma likes to have her own way. Just like me!*

Filled with this knowledge, Rosie came back to reality.

Gretchen glanced up from her book. "I see your 'train of thought' got where it was going."

"Yes, I suppose."

"Now will you tell *Hamlet?*"

"Yes, Rosie. Do tell. The way you tell stories is so much better than the way they tell them in school."

"Ugh! School! Don't mention it. It begins tomorrow."

Rosie's heart sank. No more holiday. No more relaxed good times. There was something new to face on Monday.

"Dammit to hell," she muttered to herself. "School."

3 ❀ ❀ ❀ SCHOOL

ROSIE HAD never liked school much. And vice versa. So Monday morning found her with a stomachache and dragging feet.

Her cousins urged her along.

"Come on, Rosie!"

"Hey! Pick 'em up and lay 'em down."

Finally, Peter's impatient, "Get the lead out of your pants!" And then they were there. At one of those all-too-familiar red brick buildings with the steel doors and the forbidding look. Her cousins escorted her through the door, steered her toward the principal's office, and, with a last cheerful "You'll be OK," raced off to join their friends.

Rosie stood for a moment, sniffing. *It's always the same,* she thought. *That smell of school.*

Chalk and dirty sneakers and wet galoshes. She walked into the office.

"Yes, what is it?" The clerk was a fluttery lady.

"I'm Rose Bernard. I transferred from Chicago. I'm supposed to start today."

For some reason, Rosie's statement seemed to make the clerk flutter more.

"Dear me . . . I'll have to . . . middle of the year . . . change the records . . . extra work . . . Miss Burnquist will be . . . call a monitor . . ." Her voice trailed off and she disappeared into another office, leaving a baffled Rosie to fill in the gaps in her sentence. *She talks like a word puzzle,* thought Rosie.

A few minutes later the lady returned, bearing an armful of records and accompanied by a smug-looking little girl wearing a starched dress, who was to take Rosie to her classroom.

"Serena will . . . take these with you. . . . give them . . ." Then, suddenly, she said "Good-bye, dear," to Rosie, as if bidding her a final farewell.

Starched Dress scampered up the steel-capped stairs as if she couldn't wait to deliver Rosie to her fate. Rosie followed behind, glumly watching the stiff pleats move up the stairs, and hating the girl mightily. She tried to tell herself that this school would be different. That this time she and the teacher would be friends and she would like school. But as they approached Room 205 all Rosie's instincts told her that it would be the same as always.

In her most dismal fantasy, Rosie could never have anticipated Miss X. D. Burnquist. When they opened the door, Rosie had barely a moment to take in the scene: the desks, a figure in gray at the back of the room, thirty-five pairs of eyes, a suffocating air of industry. Then the most grating voice Rosie had ever heard bellowed, "Close that door!"

Starched Dress paled. Rosie quietly closed the door. *Say please*, popped into Rosie's head.

Rosie's record was handed to the gray figure, who still had her back to Rosie.

"What is this?" the Back demanded.

"It's my records. I'm a new pupil," said Rosie in what she hoped was a friendly and respectful tone.

The gray figure turned slowly. Rosie got her first look at Miss X. D. Burnquist.

Miss Burnquist was tall. And she seemed to be

gray all over. Gray hair. Gray dress, gray eyes behind gray steel-rimmed spectacles. Her eyes never stopped moving, nor did her head. It was as if by angling her head properly, she might catch in her eye 360° of wrongdoing. That, and her beaklike nose, gave her the appearance of a large gray bird. A bird of prey. *She looks just like an eagle,* Rosie decided.

The teacher and the pupil looked each other in the eye. It was Rosie who finally spoke.

"I'm Rose Bernard," she said bravely. Her name fell into the silence like a rock into a well.

Miss X. D. Burnquist spoke. "Yes," she said, as if only by her acknowledgment would the statement be true. "Very well, then, Rose Bernard. Be seated at the back of the room. I have already begun my morning's classes." Everything she said was a reprimand.

It did not suit Rosie to take a back seat for anything, or anybody. By the time she was seated and her books were in her desk, she had developed a healthy dislike for Miss X. D. Burnquist.

Miss Burnquist ignored Rosie for the rest of the morning. Rosie was grateful. She spent the time listening to Miss Burnquist's voice, reading the words carved into her desk by previous occupants, and looking into the blank faces of her new classmates. If she was hoping for an answering look, she was doomed to disappointment. Every eye faced front. Not one met hers in greeting. She was glad when the morning was over.

Peter and Gretchen were waiting for her in the schoolyard.

"How'd you do?"

"Who'd you get?"

When she told them about Miss X. D. Burnquist, they both groaned. They gave her the bad news about Miss Burnquist on the way home.

"She's the most hated teacher in the school."

"Do you know what the 'X' stands for? *Xanthippe*. She was named after some Greek guy's wife."

"Even the principal is afraid of her."

"She hates girls."

"Well," said Rosie, "that's great. In my other schools, the teachers hated me after they got to know me. This one will hate me right away."

Rosie could hardly eat lunch. She dawdled so on the way back to school that her cousins gave up in disgust and ran ahead. *Maybe I'll get hit by a trolley car,* she thought grimly as she crossed the tracks. She barely made it to school before the late bell.

The afternoon dragged. She read, she copied, she wrote. *But at least,* Rosie thought gratefully, *she hasn't called on me.* Then it happened.

It was during arithmetic review. Miss Burnquist asked for volunteers to come up to the board and do the subtraction problem. Rosie debated strategy. Should she raise her hand, hoping that Miss Burnquist wouldn't call on her if she thought she knew the answer? Or was Miss Burnquist the type who called on the person who waved his hand the hardest? It was difficult to tell. Rosie decided to hedge her bets. She put her elbow on her desk and raised her hand halfway. It was the wrong decision.

The eye-head machine swung around to her immediately.

"Let us see what Rose Bernard knows," Miss Burnquist said, implying that she was sure it wasn't much.

Rosie walked the few steps into the lion's den.

"Do problem five."

Rosie surveyed problem five. 365 take away 268. Simple. Rosie did it with ease, and put down the chalk. The end was in sight.

"Now will you please explain how you did that, Rose Bernard?"

Rosie was surprised for a moment, but she dutifully began reciting: "Eight from five doesn't go, so I add ten, that makes eight from fifteen, which is seven. So then I add ten to the bottom, makes it 7 from 16, add ten to the bottom makes it three from three. Is zero. Answer is 97."

A small tittering began in the classroom. *What are they laughing at?* thought Rosie. *I know I did it right.*

"Wrong!" Miss Burnquist's eyes gleamed triumphantly. "Your method is wrong. This is how we do it. 268. You borrow one from the column next to it to make it eight from *fifteen*. Seven. Then since you borrowed one from the six, it makes it five. Six from fifteen is nine. answer: 97. And that's the way *we* do subtraction!"

"Oh," said Rosie. She understood Miss Burnquist's method immediately. But at the same time, she knew that hers was equally correct. And she made the mistake of saying so.

"It's actually the same thing," said Rosie affably. "In your method you're adding ten and then taking it away from the top. In mine I'm adding ten to the top and then the bottom. But it comes to the same thing in the end," she said cheerfully, "so it doesn't matter."

"It matters to me," Miss Burnquist said in an icy voice. "Your method is wrong. I want you to do it my way."

Rosie's sense of logic was outraged. "But that's silly," she blurted out.

Miss Burnquist's face reddened. "Perhaps you won't think it's so silly after you do five pages of examples for homework. And," she added, "on top of each page you will write 'I have done these problems using the method Miss Burnquist taught me.'"

Rosie checked the swear word that rose to her lips. She went back to her seat.

Just then, the dismissal bell rang. *End round one,* Rosie thought bitterly.

From then on, Rosie was a marked woman. Miss Burnquist let no opportunity go by to single her out for ridicule.

She discovered that Rosie was left-handed. She pointed out what a freakish thing it was to write with the left instead of with the right hand. "The right hand is the *right* hand with which to write," she would say archly. Rosie, furious, would clutch her pen harder and reach across the desk to get to the inkwell on the other side and think of a million bizarre deaths for Miss Burnquist.

"Rose Bernard, your pencil is too short."

"Rose Bernard, your essay is too long."

"Rose Bernard, you read too fast. You write too slowly." And on and on. There was nothing that Rosie could have done to please, even if she had been the teacher-pleasing type.

Peter and Gretchen were sympathetic. They offered suggestions of the most dramatic but impractical nature as to what should be done with Miss Burnquist. But, while it comforted Rosie to know that her cousins were on her side, it didn't go far toward solving her problem.

It never occurred to her to complain to her grandparents. In 1932 children didn't expect grown-ups to do anything about a bad teacher. If you had trouble in school, well, you had it, that was all. You coped as well as you could and hoped the next year would be better. When her grandmother asked Rosie how school was, she would answer, "Lousy," and let it go at that. But now, desperate, she tried a new strategy.

Every Monday she developed new symptoms.

"I cannot move my right hand," she announced the first week. "I think I have rheumatism."

"You've probably slept on it," her grandmother would say. "Go to school."

The next week she developed a hacking cough, and was seen to spit furtively into a handkerchief. Her grandmother told her it was a disgusting habit and that she'd better stop it at once.

"I think I have t.b.," said Rosie sadly, giving a last spitting cough.

"Nonsense," said Grandma. "No one with those rosy cheeks could have t.b."

"That's where you're wrong," said Rosie, who planned a career in medicine. "One of the symptoms of t.b. is a flushed countenance."

"Just take yourself and your countenance to school, young lady," said Grandma. "I wasn't born yesterday."

Unable to make her point with sickness, Rosie tried a new tack. All week she labored at the library, and the following weekend offered a new plan. She announced that she had compiled a list of all the Jewish and Christian holidays, and that since she was technically a member of both religious groups, she should be allowed to stay home for both. "Passover is coming up very soon," she said hopefully.

At this, her grandmother laid down the law. "Honestly, Rose, you can be so provoking! You're going to school, and that's that."

So Rosie went to school, where she suffered mightily.

Things might have continued this way all year if it weren't for the essay.

One morning Miss Burnquist announced, "Today for English I wish the class to write a composition entitled, 'My Pet.'" She made the announcement as if it were the most original idea in the world.

I wonder, thought Rosie, fuming, *if she has any idea how many compositions the average schoolchild writes with the title "My Pet."* Rosie thought of all the ones she'd seen and heard and read. "It's enough to make you vomit," she said softly to no one in particular.

"Rose Bernard will stop talking," said Miss Burnquist.

Rosie glared.

The paper was passed out. Instructions were given. The pens began to scrape and sputter.

Rosie sat at her desk, the untouched paper before her. *I can't do it. I just can't,* she thought. *Not again.* She chewed the end of the pen, shifted in her seat, read "E.C. loves R.M." scratched in her desk as though she had never read it before, thought about the animals that she would have liked to let loose on X. D. Burnquist. . . .

She searched her experience and her reading for a piece of animal lore that . . .

And then it came to her. The idea. Her face lit in a broad and wicked smile. She dipped her pen into the inkwell and began to write. . . .

"Time is up," said Miss Burnquist a half hour later. "Now who would like to be the first one to read his composition?" Her eagle eye searched out a victim.

Rosie deliberately slumped down in her seat, as if to hide. It worked like a charm. Miss Burnquist fixed on Rosie.

"Rose Bernard will come to the front of the class and read her composition."

Rosie stood up. She moved toward the front of the class. She looked out at the assemblage.

In her sweetest voice, she began to read:

"My pet. Ahem! I have the most adorable little pet in the world. It is only about three inches long. It is soft and furry and has no tail, but it has little wings that fold right up when it isn't using them. It is gray. It hangs upside down above my bed and it once scared my aunt so much she fainted. Can you guess what it is?" (Rosie paused. "No," chorused a few bold voices. Rosie knew she had her audience.) "You won't guess in a million years so I'll tell you. It is a dear little vampire bat." (Pause. Murmurs.) "Vampire bats are very interesting. I will tell you something about them. They are called vampires because they live on *blood*. The feeding habit of the vampire bat is absolutely fascinating. They have these sweet little teeth in the front of their mouths. And they don't really bite; they just slit the skin of their victims." (She was warming to her subject.) "Then they stand on them and lap up the blood with their little tongues. Vampire bats live on the blood of chickens, dogs, cows, and humans. We used to have a dog. But guess what happened to him?" (Here she paused again; she looked up, smiled sweetly and continued. . . .)

"Ever since the dog died, I have been trying to feed my vampire bat hamburger meat. But he doesn't like it, and he's getting awfully hungry." (Now she was coming to the climax.)

"Do you know my ambition? I would like to introduce my vampire bat to my teacher. I think Miss Burnquist would like my vampire bat. And I am *sure* my vampire bat would like Miss Burnquist."

Rosie finished reading her composition. There was absolute silence. Then it started. It began as scattered giggles and grew until the whole room was filled with it. Laughter. Real, live, loud, genuine children's laughter. It spilled out of the cracks in the door, danced down the corridors, invaded neighboring classrooms.

All the carefully maintained fear and discipline broke down. In vain did X. D. Burnquist shout for quiet, bang with her pointer, threaten punishment. No one listened. The children were released from her spell. And Rosie Bernard had been the instrument of their deliverance.

It was a full five minutes before there was order again in Miss Burnquist's classroom. As soon as she could be heard, that grim-faced lady sent

Rosie Bernard down to the principal.

Rosie went, gladly. She didn't care what happened now. With the cheers of her classmates ringing in her ears, she went to face her fate.

The principal got right to the point. Word of Rosie's crime had already reached him. "The composition," he said coolly, holding out his hand.

Rosie handed him her paper. He read. She waited. As he got to the end, he began to make strange snorting sounds in his throat. Rosie noted that his ears were turning pink.

Suddenly he seemed anxious to get rid of her. "That will be all, Rose Bernard. You may go—I'll take care of this."

Seeing that she was still sitting, he said impatiently, "Go on. Back to your classroom—scoot!" Rosie turned to go. As she walked out of the door, he called softly,

"And—Rose . . ."

"Yes, sir." She paused in the doorway.

"Give my regards to that bat of yours."

Rosie returned to class.

School was a lot better after that. For one thing, the old order was never fully restored. Miss Burnquist was still strict, but she was no longer a tyrant. She was the ruler, but she knew she sat on a shaky throne. And although she would occasionally make a small guerrilla attack in Rosie's direction, she seemed to sense that Rose Bernard had won the field.

When Peter and Gretchen heard about it, they claimed it as a family victory.

"But how did you know so much about vampire bats?"

"I read about them once in the *National Geographic*."

"You mean you never had one?"

" 'Course not. Think I'm crazy?"

"Oh! Rosie! Ha! Rosie!" Peter rolled on the floor in an agony of pleasure.

Gretchen giggled and shook her head. "Honestly, Rosie," she said, "you're the limit."

It was true. Rosie was.

4  PLAY

THERE MUST have been something about the air in Brooklyn. Rosie began to bloom.

"I have a lot of plans," she wrote her father. "I am definitely going to be something to do with medicine. I have bought a notebook. I am going to start a medical journal. It is called 'Mind and Body.'"

By the next week, her interest in medicine had become refined. "Maybe I will be an animal doctor," she confided to Gretchen.

"That's not for girls," said Gretchen, who had definite ideas about a woman's place.

"I don't care. I'm going to."

Rosie began to collect medical data on animals. All stray dogs and cats became fair game for her ministrations. In one two-week period twenty cats were treated in the city of Brooklyn by Rosie Bernard. But then her enthusiasm began to cool. Cats were too ordinary. She began to read books on other animals. She worked her way down the classification scale. Mammals, then birds, reptiles, fish, invertebrates.

Until one day she was saying to Peter, "Echinoderms are very interesting. Do you know that?"

"You are goofy. Do you know that?" said Peter fondly. "Come on out and play."

She did. How she played! She was full of ideas and energy. And something more. Once, right in the middle of a game of hide-and-seek, scrunched down between two garages, with a spider web tickling her nose, hot, sweaty, and gasping for breath, Rosie realized what it was. *Why! I'm happy,* she said to herself. *Really happy! For the first time since Mama died.* She had all she could do to keep from yelling it out loud.

About this time, spring came to Brooklyn. And Rosie fell in love. The boy's name was Oswald Peterson. He lived seven houses away on the same block, and owned a two-wheeler. For a long time it was not clear to anyone, including Rosie, which she liked better—the bicycle or Oswald. But the issue was settled when Oswald generously offered Rosie the loan of the bicycle at any time. After Rosie had ridden it around the block 157 times, she began to concentrate on Oswald's generosity, and then on Oswald.

Rosie concentrated on Oswald with a singleness of purpose typical of Rosie and disturbing to Oswald. She caught up with him when they were walking to school. She appeared at the schoolyard whenever he was playing stickball there. She made it her business to pass his house a dozen times a day. If Oswald happened to come out of his house on one of these occasions, Rosie would always say, "Oh! Oswald. Fancy meeting you here," as if his presence on that particular doorstep was a matter of the greatest surprise to her.

"Why does she say that?" he asked Peter, mystified. "She knows I live there."

But Peter was as much in the dark as his friend. "Don't ask me," he'd say, shaking his head.

Peter didn't understand that for Rosie, the

very sight of Oswald walking down the street in his corduroy knickers with his leather aviator's cap on his head was enough to send her into indescribable transports of joy.

"What's the matter with you, you having a fit or something?" he would ask, when one of these paroxysms seized her.

Only Gretchen understood. So it was natural that a great deal of whispering and giggling went on between the two girls. By the time the trees had begun to leaf and a passionate note had been written and delivered by the faithful Gretchen, Rosie was in that state of near-insanity commonly called lovesickness.

It's hard to say where it might have ended if Rosie hadn't been Rosie and if love didn't make people do foolish things. But she was, and it does, and that's why the whole thing was left up in the air, in a manner of speaking.

One Saturday afternoon, they sat on the stoop, talking about the movie they had just seen.

"How'd you like when Tom Mix jumps from that cliff. Do you think he made it?"

"They always make it. Otherwise it wouldn't be continued next week," said Peter cynically.

"Well, that's dumb. Then what's the use of going every week to see if he made it? That's dumb."

Many things were dumb. They talked more about Tom Mix's cliff-jumping prowess, as compared with other heroes of the Saturday serials.

"Actually," Peter said, "nobody could make that jump in real life. That must have been about fifteen feet."

"No, it wasn't that far," said Gretchen soberly.

"You could do it with a running start." Rosie got up to demonstrate. "See, if you started back here, you could . . ." She took off, landed two sidewalk spaces ahead. "See."

Peter, not to be outdone, hoisted his knickers and gave it a try. His weight brought him a little short of Rosie's leap, but no one said anything about it.

Oswald came up to join them. Since everyone went to the movies on Saturdays, it was not hard for him to figure out what they were talking about.

"It's not the same," said Oswald, "if you don't have anything under you."

Rosie thought about that for a while, as she

thought about everything Oswald said. Gradually, a nice solid idea began to take shape in her busy brain. It was the sort of idea that generally is thought of on sunny spring days when it seems as if you could do anything and have it come out all right.

"Hey!" said Rosie. "Let's *try* it with nothing underneath."

"Yeah, sure. Go jump off a cliff."

"We don't need a cliff. We've got the roof!"

Gretchen looked at Rosie, horrified. "You are out of your mind," she said. "The roof is three floors up, and this is a very tall house."

"It's like a cliff," said Rosie excitedly. "Just like a cliff. And with a good running start, you could jump across the alley to the Christianos' roof."

"You could jump across to the hospital, that's where!"

"You mean you want to jump from the *roof?*" said Oswald incredulously. At last, Rosie had his attention. Now nothing short of physical restraint would stop her from carrying out her plan.

"You will break your neck," Gretchen predicted.

But Rosie didn't hear. She raced into the house to make her preparations. The ladies had gone shopping downtown. Grandpa was sleeping because he worked at night. The coast was clear.

The word got around the neighborhood quickly. By the time Rosie had put on a pair of sneakers for traction, an audience had gathered in the alley between the two houses.

Up on the roof, Peter and Gretchen made a last ditch effort to dissuade her.

"I'll tell," Gretchen bluffed. "I'll wake Grandpa and tell."

"You do and I'll tell something about you. *You* know," Rosie said significantly. Rosie had absolutely nothing to tell, but she understood the power of intimidation. Gretchen said no more.

Peter stood cracking his knuckles nervously. "Why don't we at least lay some mattresses down in the alley," he suggested. Peter's scientific curiosity was aroused by the coming event, even though he was extremely worried about the outcome. He marveled at how things could get out of hand with Rosie around.

Meanwhile, Rosie was preparing. She carefully

paced off the roof, tested her sneakers on the surface, determined the direction of the wind by wetting her finger and holding it up. . . .

"Don't be so *dramatic,*" Gretchen said nervously. "If you're going to do it, do it and get it over with."

Now Katie arrived on the roof clutching a paper Japanese parasol. She handed it to Rosie with the comment, "Like the circus." By this she meant for Rosie to use it the way circus acrobats do. Rosie thanked her.

"Look before you leap," said Rosie cheerfully, and went to the edge to look over. That was a mistake. Never had the sidewalk seemed so far away, or the concrete so hard and unyielding. Then she caught sight of Oswald Peterson below. Oswald was her sworn beloved. She certainly wasn't going to quit with him watching. She stood up resolutely.

"Don't do it, I beg you," said Gretchen.

"Stop sniveling. Nothing will happen," Rosie said bravely. Secretly, she was terrified.

She measured the width of the roof gutter with her toe. She walked back and forth a few times. The audience grew. It occurred to Rosie

47

that they could have charged admission. *If you're going to break your neck*, she thought wryly, *you might as well get paid for it.*

Now the crowd was getting restless. With true show-business sense of timing, Rosie stepped back. "Now for the moment of truth," she shouted.

She stood, poised.

She ran.

She leaped. She regretted. *Continued next week*, popped into her head as she flew through the air. And then . . . she landed. The thing was done. Rosie lay for a minute, her back against the hot roof, looking up into the blue spring sky, and listening to the cheers from below. She savored the feeling of being a heroine.

But, like all such moments, it didn't last. She was just beginning to control her racing heart when she heard a voice from below yelling, "Now come on back, why don't you?" Did her ears deceive her? Unbelieving, she peered over the edge. It was. It was Oswald. *Oswald!* Urging her to risk her life again. And now the others were taking up the cry.

"Again. Do it again."

Only her cousins were calling, "Don't, Rosie. Come on down." And Peter was shouting angrily, "Don't you *dare* do it again."

Slowly Rosie raised herself. She opened the Christianos' window, climbed into the top-floor bedroom, walked down the back stairs, and stepped out to join her peers in the alley.

She walked straight up to Oswald. "You are a stupid jackass," she said calmly. "Go home." Oswald fled. The others followed.

Now only Gretchen and Peter were left by her side. Wisely, they said nothing.

Rosie sat down on the stoop. A hundred different feelings were flowing through her. She put her head in her hands. "That was a dumb trick," she said. "A stupid trick. I could have killed myself. And what for? Just to show off for a boy. And the worst of it is, he didn't *care*. He *wanted* to see me break my goddamn neck. He didn't *care*."

Rosie's moment of truth was hard.

"I knew you wouldn't enjoy it," said Gretchen gently.

Peter was enraged. For the first time he realized the forces that had been at work.

"I should have punched him in the nose," he said. "Rosie, do you want me to punch him in the nose?"

Rosie raised her head. "No," she sighed. "I think there has been quite enough action for one day around here."

Now Gretchen was there, asking quietly, "Want to play paper dolls? I'll trade you my Jean Harlow for your Janet Gaynor."

Rosie sniffled a little. And then they played. And that, as they say, was the end of *that*.

5 ✿ ✿ ✿   DADDY

"He's late. He should have been here already."
Rosie pushed aside the lace curtain for the hundredth time and peered out at the empty street.

"A watched pot never boils," her grandmother advised from her rocking chair.

Rosie returned to the sofa, spread her good dress carefully beneath her, and sat down. She noticed a spot on her new Mary Janes. She cleaned it off with a little spit. She straightened out her socks, retied her hair bow, and bounced impatiently on the sofa a few times.

"Rosie, stop fidgeting. Read a book."

"Well, where the devil is he?"

"And don't use that language."

"You said not to take the Lord's name in vain. You didn't say anything about the devil."

"That's enough out of you."

Rosie couldn't bear it any longer. "I'm going up to watch from the roof."

Her grandmother was relieved. "Good riddance," she said amiably. Peter and Gretchen and little Katie had gone somewhere for the day, and so she was taking the full brunt of Rosie's excitement over the arrival of her father. Rosie in a state of excitement was quite a bit for anyone to take.

Rosie went up to the roof, where she stood, like Penelope on the battlements, waiting for a glimpse of a yellow Oldsmobile roadster.

It's nice up here, Rosie thought. *If you're not worrying about jumping.* She could see all of East 3rd Street and some of Avenue I. And, way off in the distance, she thought she saw a little bit of Coney Island.

She stood quite still, inhaling all the smells of spring. Then it was there. The yellow roadster. Just pulling up to the curb.

For a minute she didn't move. She stood there, watching her father get out of the car. *How handsome he is,* she thought. *No. Not handsome. Interesting.* With his black hair, and his thin body and long legs and the jacket slung over his shoulders like a cape.

Then . . . "DADDY!" she shouted. Before Mr. Bernard could figure out where the voice was coming from, she was down the stairs, out the door, and flinging herself into his arms.

"Daddy! Oh, Daddy, Daddy, Daddy." She hugged him, smelling the nice familiar shaving cream smell of his cheek.

"Well, I do believe it's a daughter of mine. Rosie, posie, how good it is to see you!"

They walked up the steps hand in hand. Grandma was waiting. "Hello, Rob," she said. "It's been a long time."

"Hello, Mother," he said respectfully, and he kissed her on the cheek. They said a few things to each other, and then Grandma bustled off to make coffee and Rosie was alone with her father.

"Well, and how goes it, old girl?" he said. She settled herself in next to him and proceeded to bring him up to date on the news of three months.

They talked. And talked. The coffee came and went; the sun went down. And still Rosie talked. She told her father about Peter and Gretchen, about school, about Oswald Peterson and the roof, about Grandma making her take cod-liver oil, about wanting to be a doctor, about her "Mind and Body" book. She poured out all of her experiences, thoughts, and ideas to her father.

Until finally Grandma came in and said, "Rosie, your Daddy must be tired. Why don't you let him rest a few minutes before dinner."

She let him go, reluctantly, and was impossible until he got up.

That night, everyone ate together. They had a festive dinner to celebrate Daddy's arrival. Grandma had had the sauerbraten pickling for days. Now it came to the table, massive, brown, and tender, bathed in the sweet-and-sour gravy that was Grandma's secret recipe, surrounded by the light potato dumplings Grandma called *kartoffel kloese*. There were two vegetables, and Grandpa even brought up some homemade beer from the basement.

"Why do they call it *near* beer?" Rosie asked, watching the grown-ups drink the brown, foamy liquid.

"Because it's not *really* beer. It's just *near* to beer," said Peter.

Rosie tried a sip and thought it was bitter. But everyone else seemed to enjoy it.

Grandma had baked apple pie for dessert, and when the meal was finished Daddy held his stomach and said, "Mother, that's the best meal I've eaten in four months."

Grandma sniffed. "That's not saying too much, considering the fleabag hotels you stay in when you're away." But you could tell she was pleased. Daddy had a way of saying things that pleased people. Rosie remembered Grandma once saying to someone, "Rob can charm the birds right out of the trees."

Certainly the family swarmed around him that night like a flock of birds. They listened as he told stories about his travels, about how things were in Chicago and Philadelphia and Boston, and about famous people he had met.

"So I said to Jack Barrymore," he would begin, and be off on another story. When Daddy talked, it was like he was onstage. Nobody else said anything much; everyone listened. Rosie wondered how she had *survived* these four months without her glamorous, wonderful, interesting father.

But then she looked up and caught Peter's eye. He winked at her. Just as if he knew what she was thinking. She came back to Brooklyn.

Daddy jumped up. "Good heavens, I almost forgot. The presents. Stay, friends, I shall return." He went out to the car and came back with an enormous box. There was something for everyone: tobacco and whiskey for the men ("Where do you get whiskey during Prohibition?" "Aha! I have my sources."); sachet and perfume for the ladies ("Oh, Rob, you shouldn't have."); for the children, chocolate Easter eggs and crayons and tops and a paper-doll book that had paper dolls from every country in the world.

There was one box still unopened. It was for all the children. And of course Mr. Bernard presented it with a speech.

"Inasmuch as my daughter may be missing her stage life—and inasmuch as there might be a need for a little theater in Brooklyn—and inasmuch as there are actors, actresses, and stagehands available here (he looked around the room)—I thought I would provide a theater." He pulled the paper off the big square box. And there was a miniature theater. Everything was perfect: the red velvet curtain; the footlights which had only to be plugged in to an electric socket; and the wooden steps on each side.

"Oh, Daddy," Rosie breathed. "It's perfect." A half dozen puppets came with it. A man and woman, a boy and girl, and two animals.

The children were ecstatic. "We can do *Hamlet*, now!" Rosie cried.

"And Tom Sawyer."

"And Elsie Dinsmore."

"And Little Miss Muffet," said Katie clearly.

The grown-ups were forgotten. The children huddled in a corner of the living room on the floor, making their plans for the theatrical season.

A short skit was improvised on the spot. After a half hour of intense rehearsal by Rosie, the director (whose direction seemed to consist mainly of ordering, "Take it from the top!"), it was performed, with Peter providing musical background on the player piano. It was applauded heartily. And then the children were packed off to bed. Except Rosie, who was allowed to stay up.

So Rosie sat at her father's knee and listened to the grown-ups talk. Soon her eyes began to droop. But Rosie half-asleep was more alert than most young persons who are wide-awake. She picked up most of the conversation.

"Rob, do you think Franklin Roosevelt can pull us out of the Depression?"

"I hope so. I've been very lucky."

"It's not luck. You're one of the most famous actors in the country."

"But I tell you I saw plenty of actors on the breadlines in Boston."

"There are so many people out of work here in New York, too."

"Listen, every week when I go to get my pay, I think, this is it," said Grandpa.

"I feel lucky to have a job, never mind money in the bank."

Rosie thought drowsily, "They're talking about Hard Times again."

She dozed.

But now Rosie's consciousness was aroused by a new turn the conversation had taken.

"So we went to the party and met Charlie Chaplin."

"We thought that next year we would join the *Group Theater*."

Who, she wondered sleepily, was the other part of "we."

And then, in answer to someone's question,

she heard Daddy say, "She's a damn fine actress, too." Who? Who was a damn fine actress?

Now her father was standing up, gently moving her from his knee.

"And now, folks, if you'll excuse me, I'm going to take this young lady up to bed. She's had a big day today, and I'm going to have a big one tomorrow."

Instantly Rosie was wide awake. "Why do you have to go tomorrow?" she demanded.

"Let's talk about it upstairs."

While Rosie got ready for bed, she berated her father. "Why can't you have a regular job like Uncle Henry and Uncle Lew?"

"Because acting is all I know, Rosie, my love," her father said lightly. "And at the moment it's paying me better than any other job I could get. That's why I'm able to buy certain little girls puppet theaters."

"I don't care about the puppet theater," Rosie said crankily. "I'd rather have you."

"I know, baby. It's lonely for me, too. But someday—" he hesitated, "we'll be together again. As a family. . . ."

"You mean just you and me," she said happily.

"Well, yes, and . . . maybe . . ."

Her father seemed about to say something, but then he changed his mind. Rosie was sleepy and tired of talking. But even in her sleepy state she was uneasy and felt somehow that she didn't want to hear what her father was going to say.

"Come on, I'll tuck you in now." She climbed into bed and her father kissed her good night.

"Will you be here when I wake up?"

"I don't think so, love."

He waved, switched off the light, and was gone.

Here today and gone tomorrow, thought Rosie Bernard, and she tried hard not to cry.

6 ❀ ❀ ❀ NATURE

"WHAT'S EATING Grandpa?" asked Rosie, who was a great one for sensing people's moods. "He's acting so peculiar."

"Peculiar how?"

"Oh, I don't know. Like he's got something up his sleeve. He's out in the garden, humming and talking to himself. Something's going on."

"Don't you know?" Peter explained. "It's garden time. He gets this way every year. In fact, I don't think they should judge spring from when the groundhog comes out of his hole. They should count it from when Grandpa starts humming and muttering."

Rosie let all this sink in. She wondered whether there was anything in it worth putting in her "Mind and Body" book. Then, deciding that

Grandpa's actions were worthy of further investigation, she went looking for him.

She found him in the backyard, where she heard him engaged in earnest conversation.

"So, Darwin tulips," she heard him say. "You've decided you will come back this year. But you had to be fed first, yes? And you, hyacinths, I put you under the window so we can smell you from the house. And you, daffodils," he said to the yellow flowers, "you I can always depend on. Ach! Poor roses. What a hard winter you've had. Well, we will see what happens."

When he saw Rosie standing there, he said, "Here comes the prettiest rose in the garden." He put his arm around her. "Come, I will show you what is happening here."

Rosie looked around her. Suddenly, it was as if she'd never really seen the garden before. All through the early spring, Grandpa had been back here, doing things in the mud. The grass in the center of the little backyard was green, and everywhere there were green sprouts and buds and flowers blooming.

"See here, where the perennials are coming up." Grandpa poked gently at the soil with his stub of a finger. Grandpa had one finger that had been cut off halfway, the result of an old accident. Rosie was fascinated by the finger, and by the way Grandpa managed to do all sorts of things with it. Grandpa's finger, or rather his lack of it, figured prominently in her "Mind and Body" book.

Now Grandpa was standing beside the pine tree, talking to a robin. "So, old lady. Back again, eh! Coming to steal my worms for your babies. Well, that's all right. Help yourself." He turned to Rosie. "Old lady comes back for three years now. She will build her nest in the tree soon. You'll see. In fact," he said suddenly, "this will be a good spot."

"Good spot for what?"

"Good spot for your garden."

"You mean I'm going to have my own garden?"

"Oh, yes. Remember. I promised you."

Rosie was ecstatic. "Oh, Grandpa. You are the *best*."

"Yes, well, we'll see. It's a lot of work, mind you. Not easy, a garden. But it will be good. Maybe. Maybe we get started right away," he said energetically. He looked sad for a moment. "It will keep my mind off things," he added.

65

So they got out the spades and pitchforks, and Grandpa showed Rosie where to dig.

"We use the pine tree as a background," he explained. "Then we dig out a shape like so—" He drew a wide arc, brought it in toward the tree, then out again. "See, that way it will be out from the tree and catch the sun. And it's a good shape," he added, pleased with himself.

"Why don't we make a square garden?" asked Rosie, thinking of the formal gardens she'd seen in pictures.

"Nature doesn't like a square," Grandpa said with authority, as though the word had been handed down to him by the Lady herself. "This is more natural. You'll see."

Rosie couldn't wait to see. It was hard for her to go through the preparation, because she was so eager for the results.

For the next few days, she and Grandpa spent all their spare time working on her garden. They turned over the soil, dug in manure, put lime in to "sweeten" it. Every rock was taken out and wheeled away in the wheelbarrow. Until at last it was a neatly sculptured, smooth patch of earth.

For Rosie, it wasn't all labor. Part of it was

school. Grandpa showed her everything. Every bug and worm was part of her instruction. She learned how earthworms aerate the soil, and how the tiniest creatures play their part in the chain of growing things. She looked at the smallest bugs under her magnifying glass and marveled at their completeness.

Then they were ready. Grandpa drew a plan—tall, shade-loving plants in the back, and shorter plants that needed sun in the front. They planned the colors—red against pale pink, blue and lavender mixed with white. The perennials would come up every year, Grandpa assured her. They would be followed by the annuals, which you must sow from seed each year.

It gave Rosie a good feeling, this garden business. If they were looking ahead to next year, and the year after, then that meant she would be here next year and the year after. This was her home.

They worked together in the warming sun, the old man and the young girl. Every afternoon and on the weekends. And Rosie learned far more than just gardening.

One day they talked about Mama—a subject Rosie had not been able to touch before.

It was Grandpa who brought it up. Rosie had

been watching the robin building her nest. "Now that's interesting," she declared, delighted with her people's-eye view of the home-building.

Grandpa laughed and shook his head.

"You remind me so much of your mother," he said. He set a poppy plant in place. "She was always so interested in everything. Just the way you are."

A wave of longing for her mother swept over Rosie. "Why do people have to die anyway?" she said, suddenly furious.

Grandpa sat back on his heels and looked at her. "I like to think of it as passing on. Changing to another state."

"You mean like going to heaven?"

He looked at her sharply. "No. I don't. I don't have much truck with that heaven business. That's your grandma's department. I just mean that everything has its time. Some flowers, some people, shorter time than others."

He took his corncob pipe out of his vest and lit it. "But, you know, there's always something left."

"Like what?" Rosie almost whispered.

"Well, there's the seed. You take a marigold. Comes the frost it withers and dies. But the next spring, you keep a sharp eye out, there's those baby marigolds, peeking out of the soil, ready to start a new generation.

"Same thing with people. You're your mother's seed. Some of what she was is in you. What you are and what you'll be is partly your mother. That's alive. You'll pass it on. Like your spirit. Your mother was a special kind of spirit and if I'm not mistaken you are, too. A rare specimen."

"But what if you die and you don't have a seed?" said Rose, only half convinced. "What about people who don't have children?"

Grandpa tapped his pipe on a rock and began cleaning it out. He sucked at it noisily. "Well, sir, all I can say is I'm a gardener. And from my experience I'd say nothing is wasted in nature. Take a flower. It blooms. It gives beauty to the eye, right? Some poet comes along and writes a poem. 'Ode to a Daffodil.' Now that poem is a work of art. It lives on, long after that daffodil is dead. Long after the poet's dead, too.

"Take your dead fruit and flowers and pile 'em in a corner and pretty soon you throw a melon seed on that pile of dead stuff and up comes the biggest melon plant you ever saw. Now. What does that mean? It means that death helps to make life, and that's a hard thing for a little girl to understand. But it's more scientific than all that heaven talk. It means that being alive is something. And what you are and what you're made of and what you do doesn't die. It passes on, one way and another. Do you see what I mean?"

Rosie was beginning to see. "Yes, I think so. I think I understand." She began to perceive the immensity of the plan that her grandfather had suggested. Every living thing. Part of every other. Linked together. "It's lovely," she whispered.

That day they finished the garden. Peter and Gretchen were glad; they had missed her. How could their theater season start without Rosie?

Now Rosie had something to watch. Every day before school she pushed open the creaking wooden gate and went to see her garden. And again in the evening she would take a look, as if something startling might have happened during the whole day that she was in school. She watched the green tips of things pushing through the soil and read the tags over and over again. Forget-me-not. Shasta daisy. Oriental poppy. Grandpa could tell what they were without the tags. *Like recognizing someone's face from seeing just their big toe,* she thought.

In a few weeks there were buds. And then one afternoon her grandfather was waiting for her at the gate.

"Come, I want to show you something." He took her hand and they walked over to the little flower bed.

The poppies had opened.

"Are they real?" Rosie breathed, because you can hardly believe a poppy in bloom. Her grandfather said they surely were, and that *she* had grown them. Rosie couldn't remember when she'd felt happier.

The next week Grandpa lost his job. Everyone talked about his having been "laid off," and there was a lot of shaking of heads and whispered conferences in the house. Everyone was uneasy.

Grandpa seemed to change after it happened. He walked a little more bent over. And when Rosie talked to him, sometimes he didn't seem to be listening. Once or twice, he spoke to her in a strange, gruff voice. Then, one night . . .

Grandpa hadn't been at supper. More and

more lately, Grandpa wasn't at supper. Rosie decided to look for him in the garden.

As soon as she opened the gate, she saw him. There was Grandpa, sitting on the little stone bench. Something about the way he sat there made Rosie run to him and put her arms around his neck.

"Don't worry, Gramps. It's all right. Everything will be OK."

He hardly seemed to hear her. He had his head in his hands. She put her arms around him. And then she smelled a bitter, strong smell. It smelled something like the beer that she had smelled when Daddy was there. Or like . . . whiskey! That's what it was. Whiskey.

Grandpa was drunk.

Rosie had seen a few movies where people got drunk. And she remembered in *Adventures of Huckleberry Finn* how Huck's Pap got drunk. But those people were always mean and ugly. What did that have to do with her sweet, kindly grandfather? How could he be drunk?

She called to him, softly. "Gramps?"

He looked at her without speaking.

She had to get him upstairs. "Come on,

Grandpa, let's go. It's time for us to be in bed."
She took his hand.

He looked at her, dazed, and let himself be
led away. He was still talking. She shushed him
and got him up the stairs somehow. When they
got to the third floor, Grandma was there.
Grandma seemed to know what had happened.

"All right, Rosie," she said firmly, "you go
along to bed. I'll take care of him."

Rosie, just as firmly, said no, she would stay
and help. For a moment, the two stubborn
women, the old one and the young, faced each
other. Then Grandma said, "Pshaw, then don't
just stand there. *Give* me a hand." Together they
got Grandpa to bed.

When he was asleep, Grandma said, "Come
downstairs to the kitchen and I'll make us some
tea." Rosie followed her meekly. In a few minutes the two were seated at the table, sipping and
talking earnestly.

"I'm sorry you had to see your grandfather
like that, Rose."

"It doesn't matter, Gram."

"You understand about it, don't you?"

"I think so. It's because of his job, isn't it?"

"Yes." Her grandmother tried to explain.

"He's—he's just feeling so bad about himself."

"But it's not his fault. It's Hard Times!!"

"Yes, but even in Hard Times a man doesn't feel like a man unless he has a job. And," Grandma added, "you see he's terribly afraid that we may lose you. He's afraid we may have to move somewhere else if he doesn't find work. And your father won't let you come with us."

"And that's why he drinks?"

Her grandmother bowed her head. "That's why he drinks."

"Something has to be done," said Rosie clearly. "We have to help Grandpa. Drinking is bad for the liver."

Something was done. Rosie wrote to her father the next day and explained the whole situation. "I know you will do something, Daddy, and I'm counting on you."

Daddy responded by sending a long letter asking why he had not been told and assuring Grandpa and Grandma that there was nothing to worry about as long as he was working. The message was duly delivered.

But Grandpa wasn't really himself again until he got a job. Even after that, it was some time before he could bring himself to talk to Rosie. The peonies and the roses were almost through before Rosie felt that they could have one of their heart-to-heart talks again.

She met him in the garden. "Hi, Gramps. How are you doing?"

"Fine, Rosie," he said, his hands trembling slightly. "You know I'm working in the soda factory with Uncle Henry."

"So I heard."

Silence.

"Grandpa," Rosie asked cordially, "are you on the wagon?"

"Yes," said her grandfather.

"That's good," said Rosie. "Drinking is awfully bad for the liver."

7 ❀ ❀ ❀ RELIGION

ON SUNDAY everyone went to church. Everyone, that is, but Rosie, Katie, and Grandpa. Rosie watched the roast and read the funny papers to Katie. Grandpa worked in the garden.

This arrangement might have continued indefinitely if Rosie's father hadn't brought her a Bible. It was a big book, printed especially for children, complete with colored pictures. And it contained both the Old and the New Testaments.

"Here you are, old girl," her father said when he gave it to her. "Now you can get at least two sides of the story."

"Two sides of what story?"

"Religion. First part's the Bible of the Jews.

The second part's the Christian Bible. Read both of them. Then we'll talk about it."

"Which part shall I read first?"

"Might as well begin at the beginning."

Rosie hefted the book, which was quite large. "When I finish will I know everything about religion?"

"Nope. There are still all the Eastern religions. Buddhism. Confucianism. Muhammadanism . . ."

"Ye gods!"

"Exactly. But anyway, start by reading this."

As soon as her father left, Rosie opened the big book.

"In the beginning God created the heaven and the earth. And the earth was without form, and void; and darkness was upon the face of the deep. . . ."

In a few minutes, she was lost in Genesis.

After that, either alone or with Peter and Gretchen, Rosie read a little from the Bible every night. Each one had his favorite story. Peter's was the story of David and Goliath. Gretchen liked the one about Ruth and Naomi. And Rosie's imagination was captured by Moses. Moses and the Burning Bush. Moses getting the Ten Commandments from God. Moses leading his people into the Promised Land. Moses became her new hero. She started a notebook on Moses.

From admiring Moses to admiring the Jewish religion was a small step for Rosie. She began to seek out Jewish people. She discovered that Mr. Brickman, who owned the candy store around the corner, was Jewish. And amenable to conversation. So the hot afternoons of July found her sitting on a folding chair in the back of Mr. Brickman's store, digesting generous amounts of Jewish philosophy along with molasses taffy and licorice. Mr. Brickman told her tales from the Talmud, touching a responsive chord in Rosie when he spoke of matters of social justice. After two weeks of discussion with Mr. Brickman, Rosie could find nothing to quarrel with in the ideals of Judaism. She felt herself ready to be one of the Chosen People. She bought a Star of David. She forswore the eating of pork. She urged her cousins to abandon their faith and be chosen, too.

Gretchen and Peter listened, open-mindedly. But they were under no pressure to make a move. They didn't have Rosie's problem. After all, they had both been born into their religion; the choice had been made for them.

"Why don't you read the New Testament before you make up your mind what you want to be?" Peter suggested. "I think you'll like Jesus."

But Rosie was deep in her Jewish phase. And Grandma was beside herself. She still had hopes for Rosie's soul; it was sorely trying for her to see her lamb straying toward another fold. However, she was honor bound not to influence her. "I will not interfere," she said. "If the child wants to be Jewish, then Jewish she shall be. It's in the Lord's hands."

But as Rosie continued to study Judaism behind the penny-candy counter, Grandma found it increasingly difficult to refrain from helping the Lord with his work.

When Rosie announced that Mr. Brickman had offered to take her to shul on a Friday night, Grandma's faith was put to the ultimate test. But she gave her permission and helped Rosie to get ready with as much care as if she approved. She ironed her dress, laid out clean socks, and brushed and braided her hair.

"Go!" she ordered sadly, in the tone of someone sending a loved one into purgatory.

Much to Grandma's joy, shul was not an unqualified success. Rosie had some questions about it.

"I don't see why the women have to sit in a separate section . . . and the men say a prayer thanking God that they're men and not women —Ye gods!"

Peter naturally was not as moved by this information as Rosie was.

"Never mind that," he said. "What about the sermon? How was the sermon?"

"Long. A lot of it was in Hebrew. I liked the singing. And I liked when they took the Torah out. . . . You know, that's the scroll with all the sacred writing on it. But . . . I thought they'd talk more about Moses and peace and justice. . . ."

Rosie was not sold on shul-going.

"I don't think I'll go to shul anymore," she announced. "I'll just be Jewish at home."

The next day she started on the New Testament. As Peter had predicted, she liked Jesus from the beginning, and the more she read, the more he gained favor in her eyes. She started a notebook on Jesus.

"Tell me something about Jesus," she would

demand of her grandmother. "Was he real? Was there really someone named Jesus?"

"Certainly. He was the Son of God. He died for our sins."

"How beautiful and noble," said Rosie. She continued the subject with her father when he came the following day.

"Tell me about Jesus," she asked.

"Well. He was a carpenter. And he changed the world."

"Grandma says he was the Son of God. And so does the New Testament. Do you think he was?"

"Well, let's put it this way. I don't know. But Jews don't believe that."

Rosie thought about that a little.

"Well, even if he wasn't, he was a great man, right?"

"Right."

"I think Moses and Jesus were a lot alike in some ways, don't you?"

"You might say so. They both wanted to make people better, more human. You know, Rosie, the Christians built on the ideas that the Hebrews developed. It's all, well, part of the same thing, in a way. . . ."

"Then why do they have Jews and Christians in the first place? Why doesn't everybody get together?"

Her father laughed and sort of groaned and rumpled her hair.

"Why, why, why indeed," he said. "Don't ask me to answer that one."

By the time Rosie had wept over the crucifixion, she announced to her grandmother that she was ready for church.

"All right, dear," said that good lady, trying to keep her joy within bounds. "This Sunday will be a good time. It's United Church Day."

"What's United Church Day?" asked Rosie.

"It's fun," said Peter, who had come in on the conversation. "There's a big parade of all the Protestants. And then everybody goes to their own church. Sort of a church holiday."

"OK. I'll do it," said Rosie.

Now Grandma swung into action. "What about new dresses for the girls?" she suggested at family meeting that night. "For United Church Day."

What Grandma wanted, Grandma usually got. New dresses. Crepe de chine. All the same style. Pink for Gretchen. Blue for Katie. And Rosie's a pale lime green.

Now that Rosie had made her decision, she went all the way to cooperate. She even let her grandmother wash her hair with camomile tea and "put it up." "Putting up" was an excruciating process where the hair was wound tightly in bits of rag until the poor victim's scalp turned pink. Rosie made only one small protest. "I don't see," she said, her eyes watering with pain, "why I'll be any better in the sight of God with my hair curly. *He* knows I have naturally straight hair."

Sunday morning arrived, hot and sunny. A perfect day for the uniting, everyone agreed. The children were instructed to eat breakfast in their underwear so they wouldn't get their good clothes dirty. Meanwhile the grown-ups tidied up and made the preparations for Sunday dinner.

At last they were dressed and ready. "Onward, Christian Soldiers," Peter called gaily. They began the march to the church.

Katie had been provided with a bicycle, decorated for the occasion with red, white, and blue streamers, and so she led the company as they merged with the growing throng.

By the time they got to Ocean Parkway, Rosie realized that this was to be a long parade. At the same time, she discovered that her new shoes hurt. And that her socks were slipping down into her shoes. She stopped every block or so and patiently pulled them out. Peter and Gretchen walked by her side, chatting and waiting for her when she had one of her sock-pulling episodes. When she'd adjusted the socks for the twentieth time, she said, "By the way, how much farther is the church?"

"It's a long way yet," Peter said cheerfully.

The sun was now high in the sky. It was hot. Rosie's head felt peculiar. *It's those curls,* she thought. She felt them bouncing against her head at every step. *I don't see why I have to have curly hair just because Gretchen and Katie have it,* she thought irritably. Now the big taffeta bow perched on top of her head was slipping. She slid it up again. It still wobbled there shakily.

Her socks were down again. She stopped and rescued them from inside her shoes.

"I'm sweating," she confided to Gretchen. "Are you sweating?"

"No."

No, of course not, thought Rosie. *Gretchen never sweats. She always looks perfect. Her socks never slip down into her shoes. Her hair curls perfectly when you just wet it. Her bow stays.* She was about to give voice to these grievances in a most un-Christian way when she was saved from herself by the band striking up "Rock of Ages." Rosie knew the song and joined in. Uplifted, she decided to forget about her socks.

By the end of "Rock of Ages," two fat blisters were forming on the back of her heels.

"How much farther?" she asked Peter.

"We're about halfway."

Noon is the hottest time of the day.

Rosie decided to concentrate on a religious subject. The Exodus. She imagined herself walking the burning sands of the desert, following Moses toward the Promised Land. She made the mistake of telling Gretchen about her fantasy.

"Don't you think that's a little out of place?" Gretchen asked.

The dream was shattered.

"OK," said Rosie, gritting her teeth, "I'll think of something else."

She imagined herself a Christian martyr

going to be crucified. Carrying her own cross. She imagined . . .

"Water . . . water," she whispered.

"What's the matter with you?" demanded Gretchen. "What are you walking all bent over like that for?"

Rosie straightened up, sighing. "How much farther?" she asked.

"Just a few blocks."

By this time, Rosie was convinced she'd never make it. But when the little band entered the church, she was still on her feet, although her blisters were now running.

"Thank God," she said earnestly, as she slid into the pew. It was cool and dark in the church, and it smelled pleasantly of lemon-oil furniture polish. Such a welcome change from the hot pavement and the merciless sun. Her grandmother settled down in front of her. Her aunts and uncles and cousins took their places in the choir. The organ began to play. The minister appeared. He began to speak . . .

"To every thing there is a season, and a time to every purpose under the heaven." (*I like that*, thought Rosie.) "A time to be born, and a time to die; a time to plant, and a time to reap" (*like*

Grandpa says). ". . . A time to weep, and a time to laugh; a time to mourn, and a time to dance. . . ." (*Oh, I like this. But I've heard it before*, thought Rosie sleepily. *Isn't it . . . Isn't it . . . from the Old Testament? Yes, yes it is.*)

Rosie's gaze wandered around the church. The stained-glass windows. Altar. Angels. Statues.

And then Rosie Bernard fell asleep.

As she slept, she dreamed. *The stained-glass windows opened. From behind each one stepped a Biblical figure. Peter and Paul. Ruth and Naomi. David and Goliath. Now here came a woman with an infant in her arms. Was it Mary with the baby Jesus? Or was it Pharaoh's daughter with Moses? Rosie pondered this question in her dream. At that moment the back of the church wall slid open to reveal the Torah. That happened in a shul, not a church. Now there were two men who looked alike. Two bearded men walking together toward the altar with their hands clasped behind them. Walking and talking. Rosie frowned in her sleep, trying to figure out who they were of course she knew of course it came to her Moses and Jesus yes Moses*

*and Jesus arm in arm and one had a Star of David
on his back and the other one had a cross and the
music got louder and louder and . . .*

Rosie awoke with a start. Her head banged
against the back of the pew. She had slipped
down almost all the way to the floor. She had a
crick in her back. Her grandmother was standing up in front of her, singing "The Old Rugged
Cross" loudly and firmly. It was impossible to tell
whether she had seen Rosie's fall from grace.
Rosie quickly stumbled to her feet and began to
sing so loudly that her grandmother turned
around and gave her a suspicious look.

On the way home, she shared her dream with
Peter and Gretchen. Gretchen found it fascinating. "I think you've had a Divine Revelation,"
she said enthusiastically. "I think God was trying to tell you something. He was probably
trying to say that good thoughts are good
thoughts no matter who said them. That it's all
kind of one and the same, and it doesn't matter
what you call yourself."

"Then, if that's the case," concluded Rosie,
stopping for a moment to rid herself of the
offending socks and continuing her walk bare-
footed, "so maybe from now on I'll just be partly

Jewish and partly Protestant—half and half," she added, with a satisfied air.

"But don't forget," Peter interjected, with a sly grin, "you haven't read about Buddhism yet."

8 ❀ ❀ ❀ SUMMER

HEAT. It came up off the pavement in waves. The trees drooped. The air was still. The street cleaner languidly pushed a Dixie cup along the curb with his broom. No one was outside. No one, that is, but the children.

"Let's play hide-and-seek."

"Too hot!"

"How about stoop ball?"

"Ugh! If I play that one more time! Besides, we lost the ball."

"We could play school," said Gretchen primly.

"For pete's sake, I had enough of school to last me a million years. I am expiring from this heat," Rosie added.

The day was long and tempers were short.

Every game seemed to be too much effort. The possibilities of the porch had been exhausted; the games that had seemed like so much fun yesterday seemed unappealing today.

"When I get to be a doctor, I am going to invent a pill to make people feel cool in the heat," said Rosie.

"I am going up on the top porch to read," said Gretchen. "Come on, Katie. And stop picking your nose," she added crabbily.

Gretchen removed herself, Katie trailing tearfully behind her.

Peter and Rosie sat gloomily on the steps, contemplating the steaming street and the long hours ahead of them. The block seemed devoid of all life.

And then. "Hey! Look. The iceman." They watched him stop his horse in front of the house, push back the blanket in the back of his truck, and reveal a huge block of ice.

Skillfully, he cut a smaller block out of it, picked it up with a pair of tongs, and headed for their house.

"Your mother home?" he asked Peter.

"Yup. Go right in."

As soon as the iceman disappeared into the

house, the children sprang into action. Four steps down to the sidewalk, hop onto the back of the truck, put your cheek briefly against the ice, and then scoop up some chips of ice to suck.

"Cool!" Rosie muttered appreciatively as she sucked on a piece of ice. "I wish they wouldn't pack it in sawdust. It gets in your teeth. Why do they, anyway?"

"Why do they what?"

"Pack it in sawdust."

"To discourage kids from doing what we're doing, I guess."

"Naw. It's to keep it from melting."

Finished with the ice, they slid off the truck. The iceman came and went. Back to nothing to do.

"Boy, what I wouldn't give to be swimming today."

"Me, too. If Daddy were here instead of on tour, he'd be taking me swimming, you bet."

Suddenly Rosie got an idea. "Why don't we go to Coney Island? We'll all go. We'll go to Coney Island."

Coney Island? There was a daring idea! Rosie had never been there, and the others had never gone all by themselves before.

"But we have no money," said Peter practically. A trip to Coney Island was expensive. It might cost as much as four dollars for all of them.

"I have money," said Rosie breathlessly. "The money that Daddy gave me when he was here. I'll treat."

"We can go on the rides and have lunch and. . . ."

"Let's go tell Gretchen and Katie."

Gretchen was willing but doubtful.

"I don't think they'll let us."

"They've *got* to let us." Rosie could never conceive of opposition to her plans.

Peter was elected to do the asking.

They started with Aunt Clemmy. She was the least strict so they felt they'd have the best chance with her.

"Nix," she said, surprisingly. "You might get lost in the crowds. And it's too far to go by yourselves."

Undaunted, they went upstairs to pester Aunt Gertie, who, if she were persuaded, could bring Aunt Clemmy around.

But she, too, was against it. Katie was too

young and they'd eat themselves sick and it was too expensive and. . . .

Feeling a little discouraged, they trudged the last flight of stairs to Grandma. Now whether it was Peter's eloquence, Rosie's insistence, or Katie's wailing that finally got to Grandma it is hard to say. But after lengthy discussion, she said that *she* guessed it would be all right. *Provided*— and then she listed her conditions, to all of which they agreed hastily. Back downstairs in triumph to announce that *Grandma* said Yes. As usual, Grandma's word carried the day.

Off they went, armed with admonitions.

> Don't talk to strangers.
> Don't lose your money.
> Don't stay in the sun too long.
> Swim in front of the lifeguard stand.
> Hold Katie's hand in the water.
> Be home at six o'clock on the dot.

It was fun to climb onto the trolley and pay like grown-ups, and then to sit on the straw seats with your bathing bag, squeezed in between other people with bathing bags who you knew were all going to the same place that you were.

The trolley was open, and the breeze fanned them as they rumbled over the cobblestone streets to the ocean side of Brooklyn.

The trolley always went underground before the Coney Island stop. When the children piled out of the dark tunnel into the white hot light of the beach, they gasped with pleasure. They raced to the boardwalk to see the water, dragging Katie, whose fat little legs couldn't keep up. There it was. The beach. The sea. Coney. And best of all, a whole day to walk around and enjoy and swim and sunbathe. No hurry. Oh, joy.

"Look at all the people."

"Look at the waves, you mean."

"Let's go in the water right away."

"No, let's go on some rides first. Then we'll go in the water."

Peter took over the organization of the day, and Rosie and Gretchen agreed to supervise Katie.

"Now stay with us. Behave yourself. Do you have to go to the bathroom? Go now. And remember, don't wander away."

First they went on the merry-go-round. That was traditional. The merry-go-round at Coney

Island was said to be the finest one in the world, Peter told them. It was certainly *fancy* enough, with its cupid carvings and its beautiful brass pipes that played music. And a place where you could grab for the brass ring. They went on it until Peter called it quits, afraid they'd squander all their money. "Let's go get something to eat," he suggested.

They got hot dogs at one stand, corn on the cob at another. Soda at another. French fries. Frozen custard. Then a refreshing trip in the Barrel of Fun, and on the moving stairs in the Hall of Mirrors.

"Now let's go in the water!"

A quick trip to the locker room and they were ready.

"Do you know how to swim, Rosie?"

"Of course I know how to swim. Daddy taught me."

"Katie doesn't," said Gretchen. "We'll have to watch her. Hold her hand tight."

"I will."

They romped in the waves, taking turns holding Katie, who had no fear and who strode into the surf as if she had an appointment on the other side of the Atlantic. Playing in the waves,

splashing, swimming, riding the breakers, they passed an hour. At last, exhausted, they flung themselves onto the sand to dry out. They lay drowsing in the sun, while Katie dug quietly in the sand nearby.

"I think the beach is my favorite place in the whole world."

"Daddy says it's restful because all the lines that meet your eye are horizontal. Horizontal lines are more restful than vertical ones."

"That's interesting," said Gretchen.

Their mood toward each other was generous and warm. It was turning out to be a perfect day.

"Do you know what sand is?" asked Peter.

"No. What?"

"Powdered rocks. Beaten to pieces by the waves."

"I didn't know that."

"Hey, look at the starfish!" Peter held it up for everyone to see.

"I just read a book about starfish," Rosie said. "You know how they eat? They wrap their arms around a clam or an oyster and squeeze. Until they force the thing open. Then they suck out its guts."

They lay on the blanket, silenced for the moment by contemplation of the natural wonders of the world.

Katie, meanwhile, had made a long row of perfectly formed sand pies. She sat back to admire them, and her fingers went to her mouth, as usual. Just before they reached her lips, Katie noticed that her fingers were full of sand. Her four-year-old brain framed the picture of putting those sandy fingers into her mouth, and didn't like it. She stood up and toddled off to the water to rinse her hands.

No one saw her go.

Eyes closed, the three philosophers lay soaking up sunshine.

"Do you burn?"

"No. I just get tan. Then I peel."

"I get freckles," said Gretchen, disgustedly. "But Katie . . . I'd better put her shirt on. She's got such fair skin, she'll get burned to a crisp." Gretchen sat up, turned around. "Where *is* Katie?" she demanded.

Peter's head, then Rosie's, jerked up. They looked over to where the "pies" still sat in a neat row, next to the abandoned pail and shovel. Katie was gone.

"Katie," Peter bellowed. "Where are you?"

"Katie, come back," Gretchen and Rose called. But there was no Katie in sight.

Leaving their blanket to mark the spot, the three spread out.

They walked back and forth among the sprawled bodies, calling, asking, "Have you seen . . . ?" "Did a little blonde girl in a green bathing suit come this way?"

There were little blonde girls under many a beach umbrella that day. But none of them was Katie.

By the time they met back at the blanket, they were very worried.

"Dumb kid," said Peter. "We told her not to wander off like that."

"We promised we'd watch her," said Gretchen, beginning to sniffle.

Rosie saw that this emergency needed cool heads. "Let's not stand here. Gretchen, you go that way. Go for at least two blocks. Peter, you go this way for two blocks. And I—" she had immediately sensed where the danger lay "—I'll walk along by the water."

Now they raced along their appointed territory. Looking. Calling.

"Are you sure you haven't seen . . . ? She's just a little kid, about that tall. . . ." Their hearts were pounding; their throats were dry; they didn't know who to ask next.

It was hard to say how long the three scoured the beach when they heard a shrill whistle. Far down the beach, they saw the lifeguards jumping into the water with a long rope and a life preserver. By the time they got there, a crowd had gathered to watch the lifeguards swimming far out beyond the breakers. Then they saw them lift something and begin to bring it in.

"What is it?" Rosie asked someone in the crowd.

"Drowning. They got someone out there."

"Is it, is she . . . I mean is the person all right?"

"Don't know yet."

Rosie looked over the crowd and saw a white-faced Gretchen and Peter watching, too. She moved over and joined them and silently they waited. Rosie, in her desperation, began a silent dialogue with God. *Listen, if you only don't let it be Katie, if you just don't, I'll do anything, I'll learn the Ten Commandments by heart, I'll run errands for Grandma, I'll never have another rotten thought, anything . . . Please God. God, you couldn't take Katie. It wouldn't be fair. . . .*

It seemed like a year passed before the men were at the shore and carrying a still form up the beach. Rosie cried out aloud. It wasn't Katie. She was so relieved that she trembled all over.

In a moment she was ashamed of her joy.

Because the man was dead. The lifeguards worked over him, they pumped at him, they gave him oxygen. But there was finally nothing they could do. He was dead. Drowned.

The three children stood there, overwhelmed.

Then they thought of the missing Katie. Could her small body hold such an enormous thing as Death?

They looked at one another, terrified.

Then they heard it. Far down the beach. The sound of a bullhorn. Glorious, wonderful, blaring sound of a lifeguard's bullhorn. Announcing, "We have a little lost girl at the lifeguard's stand. She answers to the name of Katie. Will her parents come and claim her?"

They raced up the beach, leaving a trail of angry sunbathers as they sprayed the sand behind them as they ran. And now they were at the life-guard stand.

There sat Katie.

She was enthroned on the high wooden seat, calmly eating frozen custard and being made much of by two lifeguards.

"Katie," Peter shouted in a breaking voice. "What are you doing up there?"

"Why did you get lost?" Katie said accusingly. "You were bad to do that."

Rosie started to laugh, couldn't quite stop, and then to her horror her laughter turned to tears. She proceeded to disgrace herself in front of the two lifeguards. Gretchen joined her. When Peter saw the two of them sobbing and gulping, he felt that he should uphold the family honor. He ordered Katie to come down from her perch and told the girls sternly to pull themselves together. He thanked the lifeguards and the four made their way back to their blanket.

Emotionally spent by the events of the day, they collected their belongings and headed for home.

As the trolley neared home they got gloomier and gloomier. "Well, all's well that ends well," said Rosie, trying to put a cheerful face on the matter.

Gretchen blew her nose. "It hasn't ended yet," she said practically. "What am I going to say at home?"

"We'll have to tell," said Peter worriedly.

"Tell about how you got lost," Katie chimed in.

They did. They told all, and punishment was meted out. But, all things considered, the grown-ups were lenient. Perhaps they took into consideration the fact that Peter, Gretchen, and Rosie had suffered enough that day. As, indeed, they had.

9 ❀ ❀ ❀   TROUBLE

THE NEXT time Daddy came to visit, he had someone with him.

What's this? A tiny warning bell sounded in Rosie's head as she watched her father walk up the steps with the dark-haired lady.

"Rosie, I'd like you to meet Lydia Tremaine. A colleague of mine in the theater company."

Rosie clasped a cool white hand. She half heard a husky voice say, "How do you do, Rose. Heard so much about you, dahling. My, you are tall, aren't you?" Rosie muttered "Verglatamee-choo," and then stood silent, absentmindedly scratching a mosquito bite on her leg, and looking, as Peter told her afterward, like a perfect moron.

The truth was, Rosie was in a state of shock.

This was all so unexpected. Her father bringing home a *woman*. But if the grown-ups sensed her confusion, they ignored it. Daddy introduced Miss Tremaine as if it were the most natural thing in the world.

Looking back later on the afternoon, Rosie thought she must have said *something*. But all she could remember was watching her father and Lydia chatting away with the grown-ups and everyone laughing and joking as if the woman with the thin eyebrows and red lips had a *right* to be sitting in this house next to Rosie's father. The longer Rosie sat and watched, the madder she got. How dared Daddy bring this beautiful, glamorous stranger home with him? She became even more furious when she decided that Lydia wasn't as beautiful as Mama had been. It seemed an insult that he had brought home someone *less* beautiful than Mama. Rosie didn't know what she wanted. She just got madder and madder.

By the time Mr. Bernard suggested that he, Lydia, and Rosie go out for dinner, all Rosie's negative feelings had jelled into a firm dislike for Lydia Tremaine.

At the restaurant, the two adults tried to be pleasant to her.

But Rosie sat in sulky silence.

The conversation limped along.

"Do you take music lessons, dahling?" (Lydia was a musician.)

"No. I hate music. I have a tin ear," Rosie lied.

There was a pause.

"How's school, Rosie?" her father asked with false heartiness, trying to fill the pause.

"Stinks," said Rosie, her mouth full of food.

"Elaborate," said her father, "after you finish that mouthful."

Rosie elaborated. "The other day I wrote a composition about my theory that it's possible to feel every cell in your body working if you just concentrate hard enough. Miss Burnquist said it was the oddest thing she'd ever read, and that I was a very strange child."

"Well, old girl, it probably was, and you may be. But that's not serious. I'd like to see that story some time. Wouldn't you, Lydia?"

"Definitely," chirped Lydia. "It sounds amusing."

"It's *not* amusing," said Rose furiously. The conversation petered out again.

Now Rosie's father and Lydia seemed to agree to give up on Rosie. They talked to each other, while Rosie sat in stolid silence, eating everything in sight.

"Hey, Rosie," her father admonished laughingly at one point, "slow down."

Rosie glared at him, and shoveled another mouthful of mashed potatoes into her mouth. How could she explain to him that she had to do something to fill the awful hollow that Lydia Tremaine's arrival had created.

Finally, Rosie finished eating. She sat back and regarded Lydia, as if to memorize everything unpleasant about her. She watched her take a lump of sugar for her coffee, and was repelled by her red nails and the blue veins on her white hands. Now Lydia blotted her mouth. Rosie noted with disgust that her lipstick came off on the napkin.

Lydia, for her part, avoided looking at Rosie. She seemed uncomfortable under Rosie's scrutiny. And when Rosie complained to the waiter that the seven-layer cake only had six layers, Lydia made a funny noise in her throat which indicated to Rosie that she had succeeded in being thoroughly irritating.

The meal could not have been described as a success.

Later, Rosie poured her heart out to Gretchen and Peter. "Oh, she's awful. The way she talks! So affected! And that *sickening* white skin. And all that *mascara*. All she talks about is plays and movies and the people she knows and. . . ."

Gretchen agreed that she certainly was *theatrical*.

Peter ventured the opinion that if you closed one eye and squinted she looked a little like Joan Crawford. Rosie was uncouth in her opinion of what Lydia looked like, eyes open or closed. At last Peter brought the insults to a halt by saying quietly, "Rosie, if your father likes her there must be something nice about her."

"Traitor," Rosie screamed at him, and ran from the room, slamming the door behind her. She almost bumped into her grandmother, who was coming to remind her that it was bedtime.

"Here, here. What's all the commotion?" she asked brusquely.

Rosie threw herself into her grandmother's arms. "Oh, Gram, I just hate her. Why did she ever have to come here?" Rosie poured her troubles into the sympathetic ear and they talked.

"Rosie, this was bound to happen sooner or

later. Your father has a right to make a new start. He's lonely and—"

"If he's so lonely, why doesn't he come and live here with us?"

"You know he can't do that. Why don't you wait before you make up your mind about her. Maybe when you get to know her better . . ."

"I'll *never* like her."

Grandma sighed. "Rosie, Rosie, I worry about you. You are such a stubborn, willful child. Life is always going to be hard for you. You fight too much. You've got to learn to take things as they come."

Rosie lifted her face and looked at her grand-mother.

"Do you?" she asked quietly.

Her grandmother smiled suddenly. "You are a cheeky girl to ask me a question like that, Rosie Bernard. No, I don't. It is my worst fault, as you well know. But I'm trying to learn as I grow older that you must concentrate on the things you can change, and let the others go. And you," she added, spanking her lightly, "better learn that, too. Now go on to bed, and don't let me hear another word out of you."

Rosie went off to bed, seething.

Daddy was staying at a hotel in New York City while the company rehearsed a new play by a young playwright named Clifford Odets, who Daddy said was very talented. Daddy was one of the stars and Lydia Tremaine was in the show, too. The thought of the two of them together at rehearsals all the time nearly drove Rosie wild. She tried not to think about it.

The whole family went to opening night. Rosie thought the play was splendid, although it was very different. Very modern, she remarked, with what she thought was great sophistication.

"But didn't you think Lydia was lousy?" she asked hopefully.

Grandma asked since when was Rosie such an expert on acting, but Peter and Gretchen agreed loyally that Lydia stunk.

That Monday the whole family left Brooklyn for the summerhouse in the Catskills. Rosie had been looking forward to this trip all summer, and now it seemed particularly pleasant to her to leave all her troubles behind her in the city. The house was a ramshackle old property that one of the uncles had bought a long time ago. It had no electricity and no inside bathroom. But it did have woods, and a wide brook which had been dammed at one end to make a swimming hole. It sat on a hill, and the fields were full of butterflies.

For a week Rosie and her cousins had a glorious time. But the second week, the play closed. And Daddy came up to spend a few days—with Lydia Tremaine. This signaled the end of Rosie's good time. Everything was spoiled by *her* presence. If Lydia swam in the brook, Rosie lost her desire to swim. If *she* went for a walk, Rosie stayed home. If *she* ate, Rosie lost her appetite.

The more Rosie saw of Lydia, the more she disliked her. The more Lydia talked, the more Rosie found to confirm her prejudice.

Lydia didn't like the country. "I'd go nuts in a place like this," she said, several times a day.

She also didn't like the sun, which gave her a headache. "And it's bad for my skin," she would announce, sitting coolly under a parasol in an immaculate white dress and eyeing Rosie, who was usually sunburned, sweaty, and dirty.

Nor did Lydia like animals. When she remarked one day that it seemed a waste to have so many rabbits running around *uncooked,*

Rosie glared at her and said, "Is there anything you like?"

And Lydia snapped back, "Yes. Children who are seen and not heard."

Rosie hated her for that remark.

There was no question. Rosie and Lydia didn't hit it off at all. But it might not have been quite so bad if Rose hadn't got encouragement from an unexpected source.

She overheard her grandmother and her Aunt Gertie talking.

"Tell me, Mama, what do you think of Lady Lydia?" Aunt Gertie asked, with a funny mocking tone in her voice.

"She certainly queens it a bit, doesn't she?" said Grandma, half-laughing. "And smoke! Why, she's a regular chimney."

"Not exactly the sort I'd picture Rob picking, would you?" Gertie added, "If only she'd make a little more effort toward Rosie. The poor thing is all upset. Have you noticed her, drooping around like she's haunting the house?"

"That child. She's the limit. They'll have their hands full with her. Strong-willed little piece of business. She'll make things worse if she isn't careful."

"I do hope it all works out."

"We'll see. . . . We'll see."

Rosie tiptoed away, her heart racing. So even they didn't like Lydia. Even the grown-ups found her lacking. Rosie was made firm in her resolve. She would institute a policy of passive resistance. From that moment on she did nothing her father wanted her to do. Or would have liked her to do.

She was moody. Sloppy. Disobedient.

She hardly spoke to anyone.

Whatever conversation she did carry on seemed designed to offend. Her dinner table talk consisted of livid descriptions of operations that she was reading about in her new medical text. Her prose was laced with words like pus and vomit.

One day she heard that Lydia loathed snakes. The next day a huge water snake mysteriously appeared in the room in which Lydia slept.

Lydia was fastidious about her clothes. They were found crumpled or soiled, in odd places.

Action bred reaction. Lydia became more and more hostile toward Rosie. And more insistent that her father put his foot down with her.

Mr. Bernard was torn between the two of

them. But at last he decided to have it out with Rosie.

"You've been behaving like a brat, do you know that?"

No answer.

Softly, "Rose, what is it you want?"

She was tight-lipped and silent.

"I know how you feel, but give her a chance."

No answer.

"Will you, Rose?"

"No. I am practicing passive resistance. Like Mahatma Gandhi."

"Good Lord." And Rob Bernard, who had never struck his child, felt sorely tempted.

Defeated, he went back to discuss matters with Lydia. Rosie didn't know the details of their conversation, but she got the general thrust of it when Lydia came downstairs a half hour later, alone, with her bags packed, and waited on the porch smoking cigarette after cigarette until the old Packard cab from the station came to pick her up.

When her father appeared later that evening, Rosie was all smiles. *Her* conditions had been met. Lydia had left. As far as Rosie was concerned, the resistance movement was over.

Oddly enough, her father didn't seem to know it. He seemed distracted, excused himself early, and went to bed. Hoping for something better from Grandma, Rosie went into the kitchen to keep her company. But Grandma's lips were pursed at her in a very strange way, and all she said was, "Well, I hope you're satisfied, young lady."

Rosie went to bed, decidedly *unsatisfied*.

The next day she made every effort to compensate for the lack of Lydia Tremaine. But her father looked at her almost as if he didn't like her. At two o'clock he announced that he was going back to New York.

Rosie knew he was going back to make it up with *her*.

She tiptoed away. Her heart was like a stone. She wandered absently around outside the house, looking at everything through her magnifying glass, as if by looking into another world she'd forget how painful this one was.

She sat on the bank of the stream and brooded, wishing she had the courage to commit suicide. They'd all be sorry if they found her floating dead on top of the water, like Ophelia in *Hamlet*, she thought grimly. Or would they be? She couldn't be sure of that, as things stood now.

She got up from the bank, and walked back up the hill.

Her father's yellow roadster was parked at the roadside. Rosie peered into it. She climbed into the rumble seat and sat there, looking idly at the upholstery through the magnifying glass. She thought of the good times she'd had riding in this rumble seat. And of how Lydia had ruined her life.

The top was up. The celluloid windows sparkled in the sun. Rosie looked through the magnifying glass at the celluloid.

The sun reflected through the magnifying glass onto the celluloid. She held it there. And held it. And held it. For a very long time. Celluloid is very flammable.

The window began to burn.

Rosie sat and watched it for a full minute. When it was a bright blaze she suddenly thought, *This car is on fire. I have set this car on fire.*

She jumped out of the rumble seat and ran into the house.

"Daddy." He was there, his bags packed.

"Daddy, Daddy," she screamed, "your car is on fire."

For a few minutes it was hectic. They had to get water from the pump in the back, and Mr. Bernard, Grandpa, and the three children formed a relay to pass buckets of water to the front. No one said anything much until the fire was put out. And then, as they surveyed the sodden upholstery and the ruins of the sporty roadster, Rosie's father said grimly, "Rose, let's go for a walk."

They walked down to the waterfall, and there her father said quietly, "All right, Rose, how did it happen?"

Rosie never lied. "I did it with the magnifying glass," she said, her lips trembling. She was so frightened at the enormity of her crime that she could scarcely speak. "You see," she whispered, "I wanted so much for you to stay."

Her father was quiet a long time. Then he sighed. "Rosie, Rosie, don't you know yet that you can't always make things happen the way you want them to? I thought you were an intelligent person, Rose. But tonight I'm ashamed of you. You've done something stupid and unthinking."

"I'm sorry." Rosie's voice was very low.

"Sorry isn't good enough. Do you realize how

many people you've hurt by your behavior over the past few weeks? Do you know *why* you did it? It's because all you've been thinking about is yourself, Rosie Bernard. Doesn't it occur to you that other people have feelings? That I have feelings? That Lydia has feelings? How could you be so selfish?"

The hot ball of anger in Rosie's middle began to dissolve. In its place lay the dead weight of her guilt. What a rotten, awful person she was. Daddy was right.

"Daddy, I'm so ashamed. I'm so truly sorry," she cried from the depths of her anguish. "Please forgive me."

Rosie's father sighed. "I guess I've been selfish, too. I didn't realize how hard it would be for you. We all forget to think about one another." He shook his head tiredly. "Come along to the house now." They went inside together.

"Daddy," Rosie asked just before he left her room, "are you going to marry her?"

"I don't know," her father answered. "I really don't know."

As soon as the car was fixed, Mr. Bernard left. A few days later, he left for Hollywood to make a movie. When his letters came, they were full of talk about California and the film business. But there was no mention of Lydia.

So nothing was decided. And after a while Lydia Tremaine was no more than a nagging worry in the back of Rosie's mind.

10 ❀ THANKSGIVING

Rosie would always remember that particular Thanksgiving. It was the first time the Penny Puppeteers gave a performance for the whole family, and it was the last happy time they all had together.

Everyone had gathered in the big dining room on the first floor. The table had been laid with two extra boards in it. Aunt Gertie had washed and ironed the biggest white linen tablecloth. The good china had been taken out of the china closet. And they were using the silver napkin rings that Aunt Clemmy kept for special occasions. All the ladies had helped make the dinner, each one cooking her specialty. Rosie thought as she surveyed the table she'd never seen such a mouth-watering array of goodies.

The turkey, crusty and tender, rested near Grandpa's place, waiting for him to carve. The cranberry jelly shimmered in the cut-glass bowl, the creamed onions bobbed invitingly in their sauce, the stuffing steamed fragrantly. The sweet potatoes had never been so fluffy and light, the giblet gravy so rich and dark. It was truly a feast. "And *everyone* is here," Rosie exclaimed happily, as she sat down to dinner with her father on one side and Peter on the other.

"Who wants light meat?" Grandpa called, as he started to carve. The plates were passed. The first appreciative bites were taken. The food was exclaimed over. "Mama, this is the best turkey you ever made," Grandpa called to Grandma, who was in the kitchen taking the pumpkin pies from the oven.

Grandma appeared briefly at the dining-room entrance. "That's what you say every year," she said, pretending not to be flattered, and disappeared again.

They ate in companionable silence. But as their stomachs got fuller, so did the conversation.

Rosie let her eyes wander happily from one face to another as she listened.

"Do you think Roosevelt is doing the right

thing with the PWA and the NRA and all those other newfangled bureaus?" Uncle Lew asked.

"I think so." That was Rosie's father speaking. "Lew, we have 12 million people out of work in this country. He has to do something drastic to cope with Hard Times."

"And yet—you still see people on the breadlines." That was Uncle Henry.

"Well, give him a chance." Daddy was a strong supporter of Mr. Roosevelt.

"Thank the Lord we have enough to put on our table," said Grandma piously, coming in to nibble and to join the conversation. The talk moved in leisurely fashion to other subjects. Grandma's home-baked bread. Eddie Cantor's radio program. A letter Uncle Henry had gotten from his brother in Germany.

Rosie half-listened, basking in the joy of having all her loved ones around her. And having Lydia absent. Lydia was doing a Christmas show somewhere and couldn't make it. When Rosie had heard that she wasn't coming, she'd been unable to restrain her joy. "Hooray," she'd shouted, and she had gotten such a reproachful look from her father that she'd almost been tempted to say she was sorry. Almost.

Now she tuned in again on the conversation, as she helped herself to seconds.

"And I tell you that your brother doesn't know what he's talking about if he says Hitler is a great man."

"Who's Hitler?" asked Rosie, between mouthfuls.

"Hitler is the new leader of Germany. A *very* bad man."

"Bad, how?" asked Peter. Peter was always interested in villains.

"Well, for one thing, he's a dictator."

"What's a dictator?"

"A dictator is someone who wants to rule all his own way."

"Like Napoleon?"

"He'll probably be worse before he's through."

"Does he kill people?" asked Peter.

"If he hasn't already, he will. Dictators are bad medicine. I predict that Germany is in for a hard time with Hitler and those Nazis."

"Oh, come on Rob. Maybe you're exaggerating a little. After all, the Germans need a strong leader and that's . . ."

"You mark my words," said Rosie's father ominously. "That man is going to cause a lot of trouble."

Rosie realized that her father was very worried about Hitler. But in a moment he was laughing.

"Charlie Chaplin does a very funny imitation of him. I was on the movie set last week and he did it for us. It was . . ." He stood up, began strutting around the room. He took out a comb and combed his hair to the side, and held the comb so it looked like a little moustache. And in a moment, he was a strutting little man named Hitler, screaming and shouting in German, and looking so ridiculous that they all laughed until they had to wipe their eyes.

"Well, at least we don't have to worry about Hitler over here," said Grandma. She brushed the crumbs off the table as if each of them was a Nazi. So much for Hitler.

Now she brought wine glasses and a decanter.

"Surprise," she said. "Dandelion wine. I made it last summer when we went to the country. I've been saving it for a special occasion."

Daddy stood up. "The special occasion," he announced, "is the first performance of that world renowned theater group, The Penny Puppeteers."

The children had slipped away from the table. Now they reappeared on cue, wheeling in the puppet theater.

"Please keep your seats, everyone," said Peter importantly.

"Lights," he commanded. Gretchen dutifully snapped off the lights. There was some scuffling and whispered instructions. The lights went up in the puppet theater and . . .

The children had been rehearsing this for weeks. Rosie had written the scripts, and had bossed and bullied her cousins through endless rehearsals. Gretchen had made the costumes and Peter the sets. The aunts had nursed the little theater group through tears and artistic temperament. Now the show was going on. . . .

The first act was a capsule version of *Alice in Wonderland*, which was printed in the program as "Alive in Wonderland," because Rosie had hit the V instead of the C on the typewriter, and she hadn't noticed it until the programs were all done. "It's just as good a title and more original," she explained defensively. Gretchen played Alice.

Everyone recognized Rosie's voice as the ferocious Red Queen. Peter outdid himself as the Mad Hatter. And Katie played the Dormouse. Even though Katie had to be admonished with an occasional "Now," when she forgot to come in on her line, the audience didn't seem to mind, and they clapped enthusiastically at the end.

The second play was Rosie's original. It was vaguely based on the life of Mary Queen of Scots, whom Rosie had read about. The script was full of weeping, love scenes, confrontation, and beheading, all of which were dear to Rosie's heart. But you could hear in Peter's voice that he was a reluctant party to the whole affair. He almost ruined one particularly torrid love scene by delivering his lines and then adding an audible whisper, "What a bunch of baloney!" This was followed by several angry shushes. The audience pretended not to notice.

The third play was much more to Peter's taste. It was a pirate story, larded with treasure, plank-walking, mutiny, and bloody inter-piratical warfare. When the last onstage fight resulted in one puppet slicing another one's head off (an engineering feat that had taken Peter weeks to figure out) and Mercurochrome spilled out of the wound in imitation of real blood, the puppeteers were so entranced that they forgot themselves completely and popped up from behind the stage to ask, "How do you like that?"

The audience liked it. They "Bravoed" and clapped their approval as the actors, Mercurochrome-smeared, appeared to take their bows.

Rosie's father said he had never seen such an original performance. "What you lack in professionalism, you certainly make up in spirit," he said admiringly. The actors basked in the praise and refreshed themselves with slices of pie and glasses of milk.

But Rosie, as usual, felt everything more intensely than anyone else. Especially success. She immediately made plans for her future career.

"If I don't become a doctor, maybe I'll be a playwright," she confided to her father later that evening.

"Why not?" said her father. "Whatever you decide to be, I'm sure you'll be a good one."

Rosie snuggled happily into her father's shoulder and gave him a good-night hug. She felt good about everything, about the day, about her family, about herself and what she could do. Everyone knows that you don't have many days like that. So it was no wonder she said, "Daddy, wasn't today a perfect day?"

Her father hesitated for just an instant. He seemed to be about to say something. Then he looked down at her glowing face, and said simply, "Yes, it was. It certainly was."

11 ❀ ❀ ❀ FLIGHT

ON DECEMBER 15, Rosie got a long-distance phone call from her father.

"That you, Longlegs?"

His voice sounded young and excited.

"It's me, Dad."

"Listen. I wanted you to be the first to know. . . ."

"Know what?"

Even as she said it, Rosie already knew what her father was going to say.

"Lydia and I were married this morning."

Rosie stared at the phone as if it were responsible for what her father had said. For a moment she couldn't make a sound. Then, swallowing, she tried to rise to the occasion.

"Gee. Uh, swell. I mean, that's keen, Dad."

Her father went on talking, just as if he didn't know that her whole world had just collapsed. He went on and on. About how they could be together again and how they were going to live in California, near a beach, and how Lydia was going to be a real mother to her, and. . . .

Just then Grandma came in. When she saw Rosie's face she took the phone gently out of her hand and the rest of the conversation was lost to Rosie. It didn't matter. She'd heard enough. She stumbled out of the room and went to find the rest of the family.

When she finished blurting out the news, everyone began talking at once.

"Well, how about that?"

"Your Daddy finally went and did it."

"Went out and tied the knot, did he?"

Rosie could hardly bear the talking. Stop! Stop! she kept saying silently. If you don't talk about it, I can pretend that it didn't happen.

Her cousins didn't seem to understand how she felt about it. "Now you have a mother again," said Gretchen contentedly, as if this were the happily ever after of a storybook.

Peter said cheerfully that he guessed Lydia

wasn't so bad even if she did smoke and pluck her eyebrows.

But when Katie said, "Now she's your stepmother just like in Cinderella," Rosie turned on her in fury and screamed, "Shut up, damn you," and ran from the room. Her grandmother didn't even go after her to deliver her usual stern lecture. She just looked after her with a sad expression.

That night Rosie couldn't sleep. The next day she had sniffles and stayed home from school. She spent the day wandering from floor to floor, avoiding everyone. All she could think about was the phone call, and the fact that her life was going to be uprooted again. She was going to have to leave Brooklyn.

For the next few days Rosie struggled with her thoughts and a cold in her head.

On Monday night she came to a decision. At eight o'clock, when the adults had gathered on the first floor for their nightly game of pinochle, and the children were in their rooms preparing for bed, she packed a small suitcase and crept down the back stairs.

She had planned to leave without talking to

anyone, but when she saw Peter's light burning she walked around to the garden and banged at the window.

"Open the window. I want to talk to you," she signaled.

He opened the window. "You're goofy. Why can't you use the door like everybody else?" he growled.

She climbed in. "I came to say good-bye. I'm running away."

"Like hell," said Peter.

"I am. Swear you won't tell."

"What's the idea, anyway? What's the matter with you that you get these dopey ideas?"

"Why should I stay here and wait for them to take me? What am I, anyway, one of the puppets from the toy theater, that you can move around on a string? Did they ask me if I wanted to live with them? No. Well, I don't, and that's final."

She glared and blew her nose loudly.

"Why don't you just say you want to stay here, then? Put your foot down."

For Peter the way seemed clear.

"After all the times I've told Daddy how much I wanted us to be together? I can't. Don't you see I can't say that now? No," she said decisively,

"I've thought the whole thing over, and this is the way it has to be."

"But where will you go?" Peter prodded gently. "You can't live by yourself."

"Swear you won't tell, first."

Peter considered.

"All right, I swear."

"I'm going to the house in the country. They'll never think to look for me there."

Peter was impressed by the originality of the idea.

"It *is* a great place to run away to," he agreed reluctantly. "They'll never think to look for you there. And you *could* stay there for the whole winter if you had enough money to buy food." He was so intrigued that it looked for a minute as if he might join her.

"Don't get any ideas," Rosie said coolly. "I'm going alone."

"Now," she continued, "I need some information from you. I know what train to take and I checked the schedule. But tell me how I get there from the station. And will I be able to get in?"

Peter drew a diagram. "You walk straight up the main road from the station to here . . . there's a white church on the corner. Turn left, like . . . this . . . and walk in about a half mile. You'll pass the bridge and the water-fall . . . and . . . it's on the right-hand side of the road."

"Will it be locked?"

"I don't know. But if it is, you can climb in a window." Peter was thinking about it as if *he* were going. "Let's see. You'll need wood to make a fire. The wood is in the woodshed . . . here . . . near the outhouse. You remember the out-house, don't you?" In spite of the seriousness of the moment, they both giggled. "But never mind that," he continued, "have you got money?"

"Daddy always sends money."

"And Rosie . . . what are you going to *do* there? I mean, you can't stay there forever."

Rosie coughed, and blew her nose again. "I don't know, Peter," she said bleakly. "I just figure, maybe, if I show Daddy that he can't just shift me around whenever he wants to, well, then, maybe . . . after I come back next spring, he'll let me stay here in Brooklyn."

She looked up hopefully at Peter. Her eyes were tear-filled.

"Right. Well . . ." The two stood there looking at each other. Then, abruptly, Rosie put her arms around her cousin and kissed him.

"So long, you big fat slob."

Peter tried to grin. "Boy, what a relief it'll be without a fresh brat like you around."

To his horror, he began to cry.

By the time he drew his fist across his eyes, Rosie was gone.

The first part of the trip was easy. Rosie walked to the subway, boarded the express, and got to Grand Central Station. Once there, she had no difficulty finding the right train. She bought her ticket and a copy of *True Romances*, just because it wasn't permitted reading matter at home. She climbed aboard. Settled in a seat near a window, Rosie watched the train start and slowly pull out of the station. *Trains,* she thought, as it passed the snow-covered roofs of the Bronx, *are a thread that moves through my life.*

Trains used to take her and Daddy and Mommy on tour. A train brought her from Chicago to New York. Even Peter's toy trains . . . trains . . . She dozed.

She woke up frightened. *Have I missed my stop?* she thought. Panic-stricken, she wiped the steaming clouded window and peered out. The train was just pulling into a station. She tried to see the name, but couldn't.

Suddenly, the conductor called, "Red Hook." *Just in time.* Hurriedly Rosie grabbed her suitcase and her magazine. She stood in the aisle, ready. The train slowed to a stop. The conductor helped her down. And then Rosie Bernard was standing on the platform all alone and the train was pulling away.

It had started to snow again. The station house, with its iron stove and its bright lights, looked inviting. But Rosie was afraid to go in. *After all, I'm a* fugitive *now. I don't want to arouse suspicion,* she told herself. So she began to trudge up the road Peter had marked on the map.

The suitcase was heavy. The wind blew snow in her face, and when the snow melted it ran down her neck. She was glad when she came to the fork in the road. She remembered Peter's map and turned left. *So far, so good,* thought Rosie. There were no streetlights. The way was dark. She stopped a minute because her nose was

running, and she looked around at all the houses, every one of them boarded up for the winter. A terrible lonely feeling swept over her. *Screw your courage to the sticking point,* she admonished herself, remembering Lady Macbeth.

Now it was a matter of keeping one foot moving after the other, a matter which seemed to require more and more concentration. Just when she thought she might not be able to make her feet do her bidding one more time, she saw the two big pine trees and the house between them. Now! Only a few feet between her and shelter! Rosie began to run. When she got to the porch, she stomped the snow off her galoshes, shook off her snowy gloves, and tried the door. It was locked. She turned to the windows, remembering Peter's suggestion, but the windows were boarded up! This was something she and Peter hadn't figured on. It was discouraging.

When Rosie heard someone crying it took her a minute or so to realize that it was she. As soon as she realized, she stopped. *Stupid to cry,* she thought. *Won't get you anywhere. Better to figure out what to do than to cry.* She wiped her eyes with a wet glove.

Leaving her suitcase on the porch, Rosie walked slowly around the house. She tried the back door. Checked the other windows. Everything was locked up tight.

And then she saw it, sticking out of the ground in a familiar wedge-shaped mound. The door to the cellar! She scraped the snow off the handles and pulled. It wasn't locked. It was stuck with snow and ice but it wasn't locked! She put her foot on the other side of it to brace herself and gave a really good yank. It opened.

A damp moldy smell came up from the pitch blackness.

Rosie shivered. She started down the stairs, reviewing in her mind's eye the possible inhabitants of cellars that she might be likely to meet.

Bats, squirrels, mice, spiders.

You are not afraid of any of those things, she reminded herself sternly, as she gripped the wall and edged her way down the stone steps.

Slowly her eyes got used to the dark.

She remembered that there was a ledge that had candles and matches on it. She felt around. Her hand made contact with one thing, then another until she groped her way to the precious matches and candles. Her fingers were so cold she could barely get them to work for her. But, at last, she had a lighted candle.

Just then there was a scuffling noise behind her. Rosie turned just in time to see a huge rat scurrying along the shelf where her hand had been a minute before.

"Ugh!" She shivered. "I forgot rats. I hate rats." She walked up the cellar stairs toward the pantry entry to the house as if in a dream. "What is it that rats can give you?" she murmured. "Oh yes, I remember. Bubonic plague. If I get bubonic plague I'll bet Daddy will be sorry."

And then she was opening the door to the kitchen. She'd made it. Rosie was in the house.

12 ❀ ❀ ❀ SICKNESS

THE FIRST *thing I'd better do is to get some
light in here,* Rosie thought as she stepped into
the kitchen. She walked through the downstairs
with her candle, lighting the kerosene lamps as
she went. When she finished, she felt better.
The house seemed more friendly now, and she
felt less tired. She made a mental note to think
about that later. *Darkness makes you tired. Is
that worth putting in the "Mind and Body"
book?*

She sat down for a minute in the living room,
and surveyed the familiar fireplace, the wicker
furniture, the worn grass rug, the deer's head
over the fireplace. *It's cold,* she thought. *Got to
get this place warm.*

There was no wood in the fireplace but she remembered Peter's instructions. She made another trip outside and carried in four big logs. She set three carefully in the grate. The logs were damp but she found some dry newspaper in a basket near the fireplace and she crumpled them neatly under the logs, the way she'd seen Grandpa do during the summer. She carefully lit them. The flames licked up around the logs and after a while she had a crackling fire going.

Now I can relax, she thought. She began to take off her wet clothes. She stripped off her galoshes, her damp stockings, shook out her wet shawl. *There's nothing nicer than a fire,* Rosie thought, holding her hands above its warm glow. Then she remembered her suitcase. She padded over to the front door in her bare feet and retrieved it from the porch.

Rosie unpacked carefully, hung her wet clothes in front of the fire to dry, and put on a long warm flannel nightgown and dry stockings. There was an old afghan lying on a chair. She wrapped it around her for a robe and sat in front of the fire, hugging her knees, until a nice warm drowsy feeling stole over her.

But now her stomach was sending her an urgent message. "I'm hungry," she said aloud. "*Really* hungry." She padded into the kitchen, found a can of soup on the shelf, and set it in a pot on the fire. When it was hot, she sipped it gratefully. *I can,* she thought idly, *I really can, feel it going all through my body and nourishing me. If I tried really hard I could feel it going into every cell,* she thought with satisfaction. *Tomorrow I'll write that down in my "Mind and Body" journal.*

She stirred the fire and put the other log on. The fire blazed up. Rosie pulled the rocking chair closer to the fire and curled up with the afghan around her. In the midst of studying a particularly interesting tongue of flame, Rosie fell asleep.

When she awoke, the fire was out. The room was freezing, and the house was dark. Her first thought was, *I've slept through a whole day and it's night again.* Then she thought, *No, I've had a catnap. It's still night.* And then she realized that it would always be night in that house because of the boarded-up windows. She stood up stiffly and padded to the front door. She opened it and a flood of sunshine came in. "Now that's more like it," she said out loud. And was astonished to hear her voice come out in a strange croak.

Her throat hurt when she spoke. In fact, everything hurt. "That's what comes of sleeping in a chair, young lady," she said, in imitation of her grandmother. She cleared her throat impatiently and sang a little, but couldn't get any sound other than the froggy one. "I'd better get a fire going again," she croaked, and pulled on her galoshes and put a coat over her nightgown so she could go out and get some more wood.

The wood retrieved, she started a new fire. Then she began to root around in the kitchen cupboard for her breakfast.

"Old Mother Hubbard," she murmured, as she surveyed the contents of the shelf. Mice had gotten into the cereal and the pancake flour. All she could find that was edible was another can of soup. *I wonder if you could live on soup,* she speculated as she drank it down, warming her hands on the cup and thinking about hot buttered toast, crisp bacon, and other things impossible to have.

"I will have to go to the village later and do some shopping. That's all there is to it," she announced to the empty room. But curiously Rosie discovered that the thought of getting dressed and going outside was extremely distasteful. In fact, it seemed all she could do to keep the fire going and to keep her eyes open. She found herself falling asleep again and again. At one point she thought drowsily, *My, living alone makes you lazy.* And she forced herself to get up and put another log on the fire.

The next time she awoke she was very thirsty. She stood up, feeling a little dizzy and went into the kitchen to get a drink of water. The faucet rumbled and sputtered but no water came.

"Dammit," she cursed weakly, "they've turned the water off."

She felt that she had to have a drink. Then she remembered the pump in the back. Wearily, she slipped on her coat and galoshes and went outside. She was vaguely surprised to see that it was dark again. *I must have slept all day,* she thought. *I wonder whether running away from home makes you sleepy?* She wished she had the energy to write in her "Mind and Body" journal.

The pump was as unrewarding as the faucet had been. Not a drop of water came from it, although she pumped with all her might. "Frozen," she said in disgust.

Her need for water grew. But at last she looked around and thought, *How stupid of me*, and scooped a handful of snow into her mouth. She filled the water pail with snow and brought it into the house and set it near the fire.

Now, she thought, *I can have water whenever I want*. She lay down on the rug in front of the fire. *Just a little catnap before I go shopping*, she thought dreamily. It seemed the only sensible thing to do. It was the only thing she wanted to do. *I'm not even hungry anymore*, she thought idly.

Rosie slept again.

When she awoke this time the fire was out, and she remembered she hadn't brought in any more wood. At the same time she noted with satisfaction that she seemed to be getting used to being cold. She didn't care so much about bringing in wood and making a fire. *It's probably what the Indian philosophers talk about*, she thought. *Like stepping on hot coals or walking on a bed of nails. You get used to it. Mind over matter*.

But at the same time another part of her was saying, *No. Something else is going on here. Something else is making you so light-headed*.

With a great effort, she concentrated. Chills, goosepimples, sore throat, thirst, sleepiness . . . *I'm sick*, thought Rose. *That's it. I'm sick.*

In a funny way, she was pleased with her own diagnosis. Done all by herself, without even a thermometer or a stethoscope. "I am a born doctor," she said with satisfaction.

A moment later she thought, *Now what?*

Here she was, alone in a freezing house, with no food. No one knew she was here except Peter, and he was sworn not to tell.

Maybe there's medicine somewhere, she reasoned. With great effort, she stood up and made her way to the kitchen. The medicine closet was bare, except for a bottle of iodine and an ancient roll of adhesive tape.

"If I cut myself, I'm all set," Rosie said aloud. Just then she coughed. It was a frightening cough. It shook her whole body and left her feeling weak and dizzy. There was something else. Rosie had heard a cough like that before. Mama had coughed like that!

I wonder, thought Rosie, *if I could possibly have pneumonia.*

It was not a happy thought.

13 ❀ ❀ ❀ RESCUE

"SHE MUST have told someone where she was going." Mr. Bernard paced up and down the room.

The grown-ups were gathered in the living room, trying to figure out the next place to look for Rosie.

It was four o'clock in the morning, three hours after Grandma had gone upstairs and found Rosie's bed empty, and the note pinned to the pillow.

Dear Folks,
I am sorry to leave without saying good-bye but I have to. I am going someplace where I can stay, and please don't try to find me because I doubt you will be able to.

Daddy, I hope you will be very happy. Lydia and I would never see eye to eye, and that is why I am leaving because I don't want to give you grief. So it is best this way. Grandma, you will understand because you would probably do the same thing if you were my age, as we are very much alike. I will always remember you. And your sauerbraten. Grandpa, please take care of my garden for me, including putting cow manure on it in the spring. Too bad I won't be there to see the tulips come up, especially Red Emperor, which I was looking forward to. I love you dearly. Remember about your liver. Aunt Clemmy, thank you for everything, especially for mothering me which I need plenty of, and which you are very good at. Aunt Gertie thanks for all the laughs we had together and for teaching me how to iron. It will come in handy if I don't become a doctor or a playwright.

Uncle Henry and Uncle Lewis I enjoyed playing pinochle with you both and also learning about the Brooklyn Dodgers. Uncle Henry I'll always think of you smoking a cigar, and Uncle Lewis sorry about the times we woke you up when you were sleeping behind the paper.

Peter, Gretchen, Katie—Don't forget about me. I'll never forget you. Maybe someday I can come back and be with you again. Do you believe in reincarnation? That's what the Hindus believe in. By the way, I'm up to Buddhism in my study of religion. Peter! REMEMBER!!!

The last word was underlined and capitalized. As Mr. Bernard finished reading the note again, the phone rang. It was the police. No one had reported seeing a skinny brown-haired girl anywhere in Brooklyn.

Mr. Bernard ran his fingers through his hair. "Where could she have gone? Why did she do it?"

"Well," said Grandma, "I think it's plain why she did it. She didn't want to leave here. And," she added, looking Mr. Bernard in the eye, "I lay the fault right at your door, Rob. You should never have called her like that. Out of a clear sky. You could have told her at Thanksgiving. What a way to tell a child about something. You should have prepared her a little more. Talked to her and . . . Ah, well, what's the use of going over that now," she said, and wiped her eyes on a corner of her apron.

Lydia, surprisingly, spoke up now. "You're right. We should have talked it over with her."

No one spoke. Then Mr. Bernard said brokenly, "I didn't realize," and looked pleadingly around him as if to get some support from somewhere.

"Never mind that now," Grandpa said. "Let's just concentrate on finding her."

"I wonder what she wanted Peter to remember?" Mr. Bernard said. And then, immediately, "We'll have to wake the children and see if they know anything."

The children staggered into the living room rubbing their eyes. Gretchen, of course, knew nothing about Rosie's disappearance, but was so shocked that she couldn't speak. As soon as Katie heard about it, she began to wail.

Peter's reaction was another story.

When he was asked what he knew about Rosie's disappearance, his "Absolutely nothing" came a little too fast.

And then when the note was read aloud again, to the accompaniment of Gretchen's horrified squeal and Katie's sobs, Peter's face turned a dark red when Mr. Bernard came to the last line. Mr. Bernard looked at him thoughtfully.

"Peter, remember . . . What were you to remember, Peter?"

"That was just a little joke between Rosie and me," Peter stammered.

"What kind of joke?" Mr. Bernard pressed him.

"I don't remember."

"Then how do you know it was a joke?"

"Ah—well—I—"

"You know where she is, don't you?" Mr. Bernard suddenly raised his voice.

"N-no. I don't."

Peter was a poor liar.

Mr. Bernard tried his charm. "Come on, Peter," he said. "You'll feel better if you tell." Then, "You'd better tell us, Peter," he threatened.

Peter's mother and father worked on him. Still, Peter held fast. After a while he almost had them convinced that, indeed, he *didn't* know anything about Rosie's disappearance. Gretchen knew better. As soon as they were alone she said, "Come on, Peter. Where is she?"

But a promise was a promise in Peter's book. He wouldn't even tell Gretchen.

The men went out to search the streets again. Grandma made a breakfast which no one ate. They all sat around the dining-room table, staring at one another and not saying much.

"It's like when Uncle William died," Gretchen whispered to Peter. "It *feels* the same as a funeral."

By this time Peter was having problems of conscience, which weren't being helped by the family's conversation.

"What if she's lying hurt somewhere—the poor lamb."

"What if she went off with someone? She always was a friendly little thing, ready to talk to anyone."

It was all Peter could do to keep from blurting out, "Don't worry. She's safe up in the country."

After a while the gloomy talk began to get to him. What if she wasn't safe in the country?

What if there had been a slip-up in the plan? What if she hadn't taken the right train or been hit by a car on the road or. . . . Gretchen, looking at Peter's face, suddenly said, "What's the matter, Peter?"

"N-nothing," he stammered, looking guilty.

Gretchen got up from the table. "Peter," she said, "let's go inside for a minute."

When they were alone she said simply, "Peter, I want you to think about what I'm going to say. You may have promised Rosie that you wouldn't tell where she was going. But Peter," she pressed on gently, "you have no way of knowing whether she got there safely.

"Supposing she didn't, Peter. Supposing by keeping your secret her life is in danger. It just doesn't make sense, Peter, to keep a dopey promise like that."

Peter didn't answer. He went to his room. All day, while the grown-ups waited and talked on the phone and cried and went in and out, Peter agonized. And all that Gretchen did was to come to the door every little while and say, "Well, Peter?"

Poor Peter. It was the hardest decision he'd had to make in his whole life. But finally, about five o'clock in the afternoon, he made up his mind.

He walked into the dining room and made his announcement.

"She's up at the house in Red Hook."

For a few seconds, no one said anything. Then Mr. Bernard jumped up. "Of course, why didn't I think of that! Of course, that's where she'd go."

No one reprimanded Peter for not telling before. They were too busy getting ready to find Rosie.

Everyone wanted to go, but Mr. Bernard said firmly, "No. I'll go. . . ." And he looked around the room, "I'll take Peter."

Peter's heart leaped, dropped again. What would Rosie say to him when she found out that he'd told? But against mammoth breach of faith he weighed seeing her again, making sure that she was all right.

"Let's go," he said. And then loyally, "Can Gretchen come?" He knew better than anyone how much Gretchen deserved to come. But at this point, Lydia, who hadn't said anything, said firmly, "*I'd* like to go." And Gretchen immediately understood that it was more important for

Lydia to be there when they found Rosie. She agreed to stay home, and the two grown-ups and Peter left immediately.

When they drove up to the house it was dark. The two pines stood like dark shadows, the boarded-up windows stared at them like blind eyes. Not a flicker of light showed anywhere. And there was no smoke coming out of the chimney.

"There's no one in that house," Mr. Bernard said, in a voice full of desperation. Then he put his head down on the steering wheel. Peter was afraid he was going to cry.

"She has to be here," said Peter.

"Look!" He grabbed Mr. Bernard's arm, pointed wordlessly. Sure enough, there on the porch was a pair of galoshes neatly together. Standing so all the world would know that there was a girl in that house.

They flew out of the car and leaped up the steps. They ran in, the three of them, calling to her, shouting, "Rosie"—"Rosie." But there was no answer. And then they saw her. Stretched out on the floor in front of the dead fire, wrapped in the afghan, with her stocking feet peeping out from under the makeshift covers. She was asleep.

When they bent over her they heard her hoarse breathing and saw her flushed cheeks.

"Good Lord, she's sick," Lydia said.

Mr. Bernard shook her gently.

"Rosie. Rosie. Wake up, old girl."

Rosie opened her eyes. She saw them, smiled feebly.

"Hello." It didn't occur to her to be surprised that they were there.

"By the way, I'm sick," she said. Frowning, she seemed to try to remember something. "I forget what it is I've got. . . . I think it's bubonic plague." She closed her eyes again.

"Always exaggerating," said her father in a husky voice. "Never mind," he said, "we're taking you home."

Rosie opened her eyes again. They were glazed with fever but even so they stared at him steadily as she said, "Where is home, Daddy?" and then, without hearing the answer, she dropped off again.

Mr. Bernard lifted her gently in his arms. They bundled her in the car as best they could, her quiet form resting against Lydia's shoulder. *How funny,* thought Peter, *she winds up lying on Lydia's shoulder. Of all people!*

Peter was relegated to the rumble seat. The wind whipped at him so badly that he ended up crawling onto the floor, where he sat and meditated on the events of the past few days.

They had phoned the news ahead, so that by the time they got to the house in Brooklyn, Grandma had everything ready.

The steam kettle was going, the mustard plaster was prepared, and the doctor was on his way.

Rosie didn't even know she was home.

14 ❦ ❦ ❦ CRISIS

"IT'S PNEUMONIA." The doctor said the word with a worried frown. In 1933 pneumonia was a serious disease.

"Keep her warm and give her some of this every four hours. Watch her closely. We'll just have to wait and see."

They waited. For the next few days, Rosie Bernard was in a fevered dream world. Sometimes she came out of it enough to know that the man with the gentle hands who smelled of soap was the doctor, and that she was in her bed in Brooklyn. But then images came to her in flashes, like a penny movie.

There was Grandma bending over her, wiping her forehead with a cool cloth.

There was Daddy, looking pale and worried.

There was Peter standing in the doorway and she couldn't even raise her arm to wave at him. *What's making my arm so heavy*, Rosie wondered vaguely.

And then one night everyone began scurrying around and she was being given things to drink and things to swallow and her chest hurt awfully, and she was floating away from them all.

Then Rosie Bernard got a little worried. "I wonder," she said to herself curiously, "if I could be dying."

And at the same moment she thought, *Oh, no you don't. Don't you dare.* Rosie Bernard, who was in tune with her own body (couldn't she feel every cell working if she really tried), began to issue orders. "Pull yourself together," she said silently. "Just pull yourself together."

The anxious people watching her couldn't hear the dialogue between Rosie and her innermost body. But they knew that "the crisis" had arrived. They watched and waited while Rosie and her cells fought it out.

At last she stopped tossing and was quiet. She began to perspire. She was drenched with sweat. They changed her bed. They changed her nightgown. Now the doctor was putting his hand on her forehead and saying gruffly, "I think the worst is over now."

And when she opened her eyes for a moment, she saw her father smiling down at her and saying, "Hey, that was some performance!"

Rosie slept. And slept. And slept.

When she woke up she had to go to the bathroom. Before she could get one leg out from under the covers her grandmother was there.

"Oh, no, you don't. Don't you *dare* get up. I'll bring you a bedpan." Rosie realized that she didn't even want to get up. Gratefully she let her grandmother take care of her.

A few minutes later, Gretchen appeared, carrying a breakfast tray. "Here you are, young lady," she said, imitating Grandma. The two girls giggled delightedly at seeing each other. "And mind you don't la-de-da around. Eat it while it's hot," she said, in a perfect imitation. This set them giggling again and then, while Rosie was eating, she caught up on the news.

"What was my temperature?"

"106."

"Wow. Then I must have almost died."

"Yup. The doctor says you were *that* close."

"Was I delirious?"

"Raving like a maniac."

"What was my pulse? What was the worst it was?"

"Oh, heavens, I don't know. You'll have to ask the doctor about that."

Rosie wanted every detail of her illness. It would make fine material for her "Mind and Body" book. In fact, the more she thought about it the more it seemed like an extremely interesting chapter.

Satisfied, she polished off her breakfast.

"Where is everybody?" she asked when she was finished scraping the last bit of egg up with her toast.

"All waiting downstairs to see you."

"I want them now."

Grandma reappeared. "Only for a few minutes. You have to have lots of rest. Don't tire yourself."

They came up, one or two at a time, and Rosie lay back among the pillows, like a queen receiving her court.

Only with Daddy and Lydia did she feel awkward. There was something she should have said, she knew. But she couldn't seem to say it. And neither could they.

Her visitors left. She slept again. When she woke up, it was time for lunch. Grandma brought the tray this time, and Rosie regarded it hungrily. Wow. Floating Island for dessert. "Gram, did you make that just for me?"

"Well, of course. Got to get you back on your feet. Floating Island's very nourishing. Full of healthy things."

"Grandma," said Rosie, when she'd satisfied her hunger, "what's going to happen when I do get back on my feet?" There was an edge of worry in her voice.

Grandma got very brisk. "Never you mind about that. You just think about getting well. One thing at a time." She swept the conversation away the same way she might have brushed cobwebs off the ceiling during spring cleaning.

Actually, Rosie didn't want to think about the future. It was pleasanter to lie here being waited on, and to have everything warm and loving and familiar around her. Maybe, she thought fleetingly, I can stay like this forever. An invalid.

But Rosie didn't really want that. She wanted to get well. She concentrated on getting well. And, as usual, with the things Rosie concentrated on, she did a pretty fine job. Every day found her stronger. Meanwhile, she spent her time writing in her "Mind and Body" book, reading, playing checkers and cards with whoever was available to help entertain her, and talking to her grandmother.

One day her grandmother said casually, "You'll certainly be home from school until after the first of the year, anyway. The holidays will give you a good chance to recuperate. Anyway," she added smiling, "I like to have you around."

Rosie looked hard at her grandmother. Was today the day she would bring up the thing they were both avoiding? *I'll have to do it myself*, she thought suddenly.

"How much longer *am* I going to be around here?" Rosie suddenly blurted out the question.

Her grandmother looked at her sharply, then looked down at her sewing again.

"I don't know, Rosie," she said quietly.

Rosie watched the needle go in and out of the fabric in Grandma's hand. Then she said, weakly,

"I suppose I'm going to have to go with them, aren't I?"

"I suppose you are." The stitching went on.

"You don't want me to stay here, right?"

Grandma stopped sewing. She looked up. "Rosie," she said, with such love in her voice that Rosie felt ashamed, "You know it isn't that. But your father loves you, too. A child's place is with her parents.

"And there's another thing," she continued as though she'd given this subject a great deal of thought, "Just remember—Grandpa and I aren't getting any younger. We're not going to be around forever. We may move back to the country anyway." Her voice went on, reasoning, explaining. *Giving excuses,* thought Rosie.

"I could stay with Aunt Clemmy and Uncle Henry and Peter."

"No, Rosie. It wouldn't work out."

"I could stay with Aunt Gertie and Uncle Lew."

"They have their own family to take care of. . . . You have a father of your own. . . . And now you have a mother of your own. . . ."

The needle raced to its destination, poking holes in the fabric. Rosie saw clearly that

Grandma was saying to her, *This is it. It has to be.*

"I don't think I can stand it," Rosie said honestly.

Grandma laid down her sewing. She looked Rosie straight in the eye. "Oh yes, you can," she said. Now they were facing each other, these two people so much alike. Grandma spoke firmly.

"Life is like that. Not always easy. Hard Times. You have to make the best of it. That's what makes you strong. And you *will* be strong. I want you to be." She paused as if to think about it some more. "I get some of my strength from my religion. But if that isn't your way, it isn't. That's all there is to it. So just look for the strength inside yourself. You'll find it. You have to."

Now she stood over Rosie as if she could give her some of the strength from her strong body. Rosie put herself in the familiar arms and did that rare thing, for her. She cried.

Grandma rocked her and crooned softly. "There, there. Think about the other person, it'll make it easier. Just think how it is for Lydia. Try to put yourself in her place. She gets married, and right away she has a grown-up child. That's her Hard Time. And your Daddy. You mustn't make him feel that he's in the middle. Rosie, do you hear what I'm saying?"

Rosie heard. She heard from somewhere deep inside of her. And she knew enough to listen hard to what her grandmother was telling her.

15 ❀ ❀ DEPARTURE

WHEN HER father and Lydia came that night, Rosie was ready. She combed her hair, put on a fresh nightgown and a pretty robe. She greeted them with a cheerful smile.

"Hi, you two. How's everything?" Rosie began to talk fast and nervously, saying the first things that popped into her head.

"D'you know I grew two inches and lost fifteen pounds while I was sick? I'm five feet five now and I weigh eighty-nine. What a freak!

"D'you know that some of the medicine I had when I was sick had opium in it?

"Lydia, want to see the potholder I'm making? It's for you. Grandma's helping me.

"By the way, thanks for the books. I read them all already."

Rosie rattled on, determined to try to bridge the gap between her and Lydia. At first Lydia didn't say much. But gradually she began to relax. For the first time, she and Rosie talked.

"Where did you live when you were a little girl, Lydia?"

"In New Jersey. Newark."

"Do you have any brothers or sisters?"

"No. I'm an only child. Like you," she added.

She told Rosie about her childhood. About how she'd gone to dancing school and to voice lessons and to piano lessons. How she'd spent all her time preparing to be in the theater.

"But didn't you have any friends? Any kids your own age?"

"Not many," Lydia said. "You see, my mother was determined that I was going to be an actress . . . and I didn't know that there was any other way to live . . . so . . ." she shrugged . . . "so here I am."

Poor Lydia, thought Rosie. No wonder she doesn't know much about kids. She never had a childhood! Suddenly Rosie felt the first stirring of sympathy and warmth toward her stepmother.

"But didn't you want to be an actress?" Rosie asked.

"Oh, I guess after a while, maybe. After all it was the only thing I knew. But the point is, I never had a chance to think about it. I didn't have any *choice*. . . .

"That's why," Lydia continued, "I—we—thought that maybe I'd quit the theater for a while and—ah—stay home with . . ." she hesitated . . . "with the family. Sort of—you know—try a new role. Try being a mother," she finished softly.

Rosie didn't say anything for a minute. She looked at Lydia closely. Lydia had circles under her eyes. She was pale. Rosie thought, Grandma's right. This is as hard for her as it is for me.

Well, she thought, *I guess this is as good a time as any.* She took a deep breath. It was like when she'd jumped from the roof.

"Say," she said brightly, "that reminds me. What are our plans?"

"What do you mean, Rosie?" her father asked.

"I mean, when are we moving to California?"

Lydia and Rosie's father looked at each other.

Her father cleared his throat. "How does the end of the month sound?"

"Sounds good to me," said Rosie promptly. "What do you think, Lydia?"

"Yes, oh yes," Lydia said faintly. "That's fine with me. I—I'll start to get things ready."

"Good. Then that's settled. I'll go tell the kids." Rosie stood up, gave her bathrobe belt a decisive yank, and walked out of the room. *You will not cry,* she ordered herself, and shoved a piece of hair into her mouth, just in case.

Her cousins were incredulous. "Why? Why?" Gretchen sobbed. "You promised you'd never go. You could stay with us. I could ask my mother. I'm sure it would be all right. Rosie," she wailed, "if you go my heart will break."

"Baloney," said Rosie shortly. "The human heart is made of muscle tissue. It can't break."

Peter was just as unbelieving. His view was that Rosie's decision represented surrender. "After all that trouble you went to," he said bitterly. "You could have *made* them leave you here. You had to go soft at the last minute. Won the battle and lost the war, that's what you did."

It was a very hard conversation for Rosie. But

she survived it. And she managed finally to convince her cousins that she was going.

The next weeks were busy. There was Christmas. And packing. And plans to be made. They tried to pretend to one another that everything was just the same as always. But as they performed each ritual they all knew it would be the last time they did it together. It gave a special poignance to the presents, the cookie-baking, the decorating of the tree.

The passage of time became the most taboo subject in the household.

And then all of a sudden Christmas and New Year's Day were over. The tree had been taken down. It was the day Rosie was to leave.

"Everything around this house says *end*, *windup*, *finish*," Rosie said sadly, as she looked out of the window where the once beautiful tree rested against a garbage can, waiting to be carted away.

She dressed slowly. New skirt, new velvet top, new rayon stockings. She brushed her hair carefully. She checked her bags to make sure she hadn't forgotten anything.

Now everyone was drifting into her room.

Each one with a different excuse. "Rosie, do you have a needle and thread?" "Rose, may I borrow that magazine you were reading?" "Rose, how nice you look." They lingered, staring morosely at her.

"Say, what is this?" Rosie said suddenly, looking around. They stared back at her helplessly. Her dear ones. The aunts. Uncle Henry and Uncle Lew. Peter and Gretchen and Katie. Grandma and Grandpa. She almost broke down.

"For pete's sake," she said, almost pleadingly. "I hate lingering farewells," she said, her voice breaking.

So they left her alone, and everyone got very busy until the old Oldsmobile roadster pulled up to the door.

How do you say good-bye? Rosie played it by ear. Everyone gathered on the porch, and she kissed each one, dry-eyed. There was an awkward moment of quiet. Then before anyone could say one of the sentimental things you usually say to someone who's leaving you, Rosie's long legs were running down the steps and she was stepping into the car.

As the car pulled away from the curb and

started down the snowy street, Rosie turned to her father and to her stepmother.

Her father leaned over and put his hand on her knee.

"It'll be all right, kiddo. Really it will."

Rosie drew in her breath. "You sure?"

"Sure. It's like a new play. Opening night jitters. But once you get onstage, you'll be OK."

Rosie looked at both of them steadily, her green eyes large in her thin face. Now her eyes were pleading.

"Do you think we'll have a long run?" she asked, with a catch in her voice. Lydia reached out and put her arm around Rosie.

"I think," she said softly, "that we have a hit on our hands."

And that was the way Rosie Bernard left Brooklyn.